Wicked Distractions

WICKED SECRETS

ANGELA ADDAMS

WICKED
SECRETS

Dedication

To all the redheads.
Burn bright. Stay sassy.

Chapter One

If Sam Henderson died this very moment, it would be the death of a sexually frustrated man.

Sitting across from him was the object of his lust—the object of lust for thousands of men—and she was completely out of his league.

"Should we go with an easy question this time or a hard one?" Despite his cool exterior, Sam's heart was pummeling his chest wall. His body was tight, and not just because his cock was already straining against his zipper. He was taut like elastic that was primed and ready for release.

Lexi Monroe, one of Sabine Cowan's most popular Kitty Cats, sat in front of him appearing more gorgeous up close than she had in her promo videos—and that was saying a lot. A natural redhead, she was stunning to look at with her pale skin and freckles. She had pink, pouty lips that begged to be kissed and intense blue eyes that could cut a guy in half if he were the kind of guy who got flustered around beautiful women—which, apparently right now, Sam was.

"I like it hard, Sam." Lexi twitched her lips into a wry grin, like a cat about to pounce on prey. "You've been teasing me all morning. Hit me with the hard stuff."

I like it hard, Sam.

He groaned silently. He'd love to give it to her hard, right here, right now. He'd throw her over the back of that chair and pound her until she moaned.

Buying himself some time, he reached up and stroked his beard then glanced at his phone and his list of questions. "Why don't you tell us what led to your decision to leave the Kitty Cats?"

When he looked up at her, she was staring intently at him, her focus shifting from him stroking his beard to his eyes. She bit her bottom lip and his whole body coiled tighter.

"She won't be answering any questions about her decision to leave the Cats, Sam." Adam, the security guard from hell, didn't even look up from his phone when Sam snapped an angry look his way. "Or about the accident. I know Sabine set out her expectations with you."

Fuck!

Sam prided himself on getting all the dirt, and so far in their long friendship, Sabine had blocked him from almost all the secrets she held, which extended right now to Lexi's secrets as well.

He was no fool. He knew both Sabine and Lexi possessed some doozies. Sabine had built her empire on them, he was sure. But that was speculation on his part, because Sam wasn't allowed to ask Lexi anything that could, even in some obscure way, uncover anything Sabine didn't want to be leaked.

Which was why he'd been so damn surprised to receive a summons from the Queen of Sex herself to do an interview with one of her most beloved Kitty Cats.

Lexi was an athlete, a gymnast, a talented one too — or had been up until a year and half ago, when she'd somehow fallen wrong and had broken things that had required multiple surgeries and a lot of physiotherapy. It was another Lexi secret Sam had planned to dig into, but apparently that was not going to happen either.

"All right." Sam shook his head as he scrolled through the list of questions Sabine had approved. "What would an aspiring Kitty Cat need to do to reach the level of success you have?" He looked up from his phone to find her staring at him again. This time, her gaze was roving over his chest and down one of his arms. She was obviously checking out his ink, and he had to admit that he liked the trail of heat her eyes left as she gave him a good once-over.

"Well, I guess…" Lexi's voice was wispy, like she was distracted by something she found intriguing. She slowly shifted her gaze back up his body until she met his eyes, sending a jolt straight to his groin. "I suppose you should be open to all possibilities — and you need to be a people person. An aspiring Kitty Cat has to be loyal and really, really good at listening."

"I've heard that you're one of the best." Sam clicked his phone off. This was not going the way he'd thought it would. "Which is why it's so surprising that you're leaving."

Adam grumbled. Sam lifted his hand to wave him off.

"Sometimes you just have to move on." Lexi shrugged, a gesture that looked practiced and full of shit. "It's time to pursue other things."

Sam leaned closer, intrigued by the look in Lexi's eyes. She was lying—that was obvious—but was she lying more to herself or to him? She shifted her eyes to her lap and Sam felt it like a wall coming down between them.

When Sabine had asked Sam to interview Lexi as a farewell expose because the successful Kitty was hanging up her cat ears and calling it quits, he'd had a dozen ideas of how to make the piece explosive. So far, Sam's questions had mostly been thwarted either by Lexi side-stepping and giving a less-than-intriguing response or Adam outright forbidding an answer. Sabine had wanted Sam to put together a fitting tribute as a farewell for her precious Kitty Cat, but that was looking more and more impossible, thanks to how secretive everyone was being. Sam had already lined up a trendy magazine to take this story, but right now he was honestly thinking that he'd have to back out of that contract, because he was getting nothing juicy to work with.

Sam sat back in his seat and draped his arm along the top of the couch.

Lexi had her hands in her lap, busy plucking with her fingers at invisible lint or something. *Am I making her nervous? Or is she uncomfortable being interviewed?* Sam had watched Lexi's promo videos many, many times. He'd researched all the interviews she'd given over the years—which hadn't been many, but still, in all that footage Lexi had been vivacious, outgoing and always smiling. The woman who sat with him now was a very subdued version of her former self.

"Tell me your most scandalous story, Lexi." Sam leaned in closer, like they were old friends sharing secrets. He had to pull something tantalizing from this interview.

She flattened her hands on her lap then looked at him with her startling eyes and, once again, he felt like she'd harpooned him and was reeling him closer.

She smelled like apples and cinnamon, and that made his mouth water.

"Give me a secret no one knows. I promise I won't tell anyone." He winked.

She laughed, tilting her head back, her hair brushing over her shoulders. Her skin was so soft-looking, and he had the most impulsive urge to reach out and stroke along her arm.

When she looked at him again, her eyes sparkled with mischief, but only for a moment. Adam cleared his throat and she shuttered herself from Sam once again.

"If I told you that, I'd have to kill you." Her gaze drifted to the windows. "You know I can't tell you that kind of thing."

Fuck, Sabine did know how to pick the loyal ones.

Lexi snapped her eyes back to meet his and she had a quirk of a smile on her lips, making him feel like she was playing him in some way he couldn't figure out. Her eyes were alight with a wickedness that made his cock harden like cement. She leaned forward, almost beckoning him to move even closer to her…like she was about to tell him a secret after all.

Twenty seconds of intensity passed where neither one of them said a word, yet Sam's senses were piqued and his body revved like he was hitting the gas, even though he had nowhere to go. He wanted to touch her, taste her. He wanted to hear her moan.

She leaned back first, putting distance between them, and Sam swayed toward her. *This woman is pure magic.*

He cleared his throat. "All right, then tell me what you look for in a man. What kind of bachelor might have some luck with a beauty like you?" He ran his fingers over his beard again, partly to disguise his embarrassment at asking such an amateur question and partly because he could tell that she liked it when he stroked his beard.

"Oh, I don't know...funny, intelligent, hard-working."

"Oh, come on, Lexi. That's not even an answer." Sam kept his tone light, like he was joking, when in reality he was dying to know the kind of guy who would attract a girl like her. "You might as well describe half the guys in the world."

She snapped her eyes up and grinned that wicked grin. "Only half?"

He barked a laughed. He liked her sass. He wanted more.

The interview carried on like that for another twenty minutes, and Sam learned about her younger years as a gymnast, the time predating her Kitty Cat life. It was clear to him that she was an athlete at heart and that whatever had happened to her with the accident, and after, had destroyed a part of her in a devastating way.

Sam badly wanted to dig into that, to find out the details surrounding the mystery of her incident, but he knew he wouldn't be getting that information from Lexi.

"Time's up." Adam walked closer, tapping at his phone without looking up. "Lexi has an appointment."

"I think I've got everything I need," Sam lied. He didn't want to upset Lexi by saying he had no idea what the point of this interview even was. She'd given him nothing, and it was Sabine's fault. She'd trained her Kitty Cats to be expert secret keepers.

Adam nodded once then turned and headed to the door. Lexi picked up her small purse then stood. Sam stood as well, not sure if he should shake Lexi's hand or what. Suddenly everything seemed very awkward.

"Thank you, Sam." She closed the distance between them.

Lexi was tall, which was unusual for a gymnast and something that she'd talked about in other interviews he'd watched. Her height had been held against her at times in competitions. Of course, she was a decorated gymnast, so she'd proven them wrong in the end, but still, she was supermodel tall, which was something Sam liked a lot. She was lithe and, of course, moved with grace. Sam could stare at her body for hours, mesmerized by how she seemed to float.

She sidled up close to him and invaded all his senses at once. Her body radiated heat, her pupils dilated, her breath, which was as fresh as mint, was hot against his neck. He froze, not wanting to scare her away, but inside he was a volcano of lust, his blood bubbling with desire. The chemistry between them was combustible.

Lexi put her hand on his forearm and leaned in so that her body was practically pressed against his. He could swear he felt her nipples bud against his forearm. Her luscious smell went straight up his nose to short-circuit his brain. She brushed her lips against his ear and whispered, "I've always had a thing for beards and tattoos. Maybe I'll see you around."

His cock pulsed, a reminder of his aching erection, and it took everything in his power not to chase after her as she walked away. He listened to her heels click on the foyer tiles.

"You've got the suite for the rest of the night, Sam. Checkout is eleven tomorrow," Adam said just before the door whooshed shut.

Sam blew out a breath then ran his hand through his hair. He tugged it free from the tie that bound it at his neck.

Lexi had secrets…big ones. What Sam wouldn't give to peel back the layers of that fine creature. He had to figure out a way to get close to her again.

Right now, he needed a cold shower—or maybe he needed to indulge himself and rub one off in a hot one instead.

He had his clothes off in record time and was under the hot spray, lathering himself up, his thoughts cycling around Lexi's sexy voice. "*I've always had a thing for beards and tattoos.*" He groaned as he took his cock in hand and began to stroke himself. "*Maybe I'll see you around.*" Fuck, yes, he'd be seeing her again. He wanted to rub his beard all over her body. He'd die to have her trace his tattoos with her tongue.

He'd love to take Lexi from behind, gather her hair in one of his hands and pound her sweet pussy until she screamed. He'd give anything for the chance to lick along every cut and angle of muscle her gorgeous body had until she moaned his name.

His balls tightened and he increased his stroking, applying pressure and letting his mind wander to how good it would feel to have Lexi's mouth wrapped around his dick. He'd stretch her lips out and he could practically feel the barrier of her throat holding him back until, slowly and steadily, she took him all the way down.

His cum exploded like a fire hose, and he painted the wall of the shower with it. The release felt great—better than great—but it did nothing to abate his desire for Lexi or the ever-cycling thoughts about stripping her down and getting her naked—physically, but also mentally. He wanted to know what made a woman like that tick and he would love a second chance, without an audience, so that he could get to know her more intimately.

But women like Lexi were unavailable to guys like Sam. He was damaged goods, running away from his past—if only because he hated what his family stood for and wanted to put as much distance between his life and theirs as he could. Lexi wasn't the only one with secrets.

He got himself rinsed off and cleaned up, then got out of the shower and toweled off. His tattoos looked darker when his skin was wet, more vibrant too. He took a minute to appraise his ink. Lexi liked tattoos, and that gave him a surprising jolt of pride. He didn't have any room left on his arms, shoulders or upper chest, but he'd been planning to add some script to his stomach as soon as he had time to spare. Maybe he'd get that going while he was in Miami.

Lexi's farewell Kitty Cat party was happening the next night and he could swing for another couple of days in Florida if it gave him the opportunity to do some recon. Obviously, he didn't have an invite, but that had never stopped him before.

He continued drying off, noting that he still had a semi and could probably go a few more rounds with his hand to fully satiate himself. Now that he'd decided he'd be seeing Lexi again, he kind of wanted to hold off, to deny himself until he figured out how to get close to her.

He left the bathroom butt-naked and found his personal, non-work cell phone. There was one guy he knew would absolutely be at Lexi's farewell party, and luckily he was an old friend who owed him one. He searched his contacts. He only used this phone on the rare occasion that he needed or desired to touch base with his past life. It had come in handy a time or two to set aside his reporter identity in favor of his actual one. He found the name he was looking for and hit Call.

"Samuel Dove, holy shit, man! How are you?" Devon Caldone was filthy rich—maybe not quite as filthy rich as the Dove family, but up there in terms of having a ridiculous amount of money, more now because of his celebrity status. Devon was a couple of years younger, but they'd gone to school together and he and Sam had been friends of sorts. They'd gone to the same parties, played the same sports, even ended up at the same university and pledged the same fraternity.

"I'm good, man. How are things with you?"

"Never been better! I'm in Miami right now, soaking up the sun, hanging with my girls. Where are you?"

"Miami too, actually."

"No fucking way! We need to catch up."

"Yeah, we do. Hey, listen... I heard you're into those Kitty Cat parties. Do you know if there's one coming up? I'd like to check it out if they're as good as I've heard."

"Oh, do I know of one? Hell yes! Tomorrow night, dude! I'll get you in with my crew! It'll be like old times. I'll send a limo. Where are you staying?"

"The Grand."

Devon whistled. "Of course you are. Only the best for my man, right?" He laughed to himself. "Okay, dude, we'll swing by to get you around ten. Sound good?"

"Great. Thanks. I'll catch you later." Sam hung up, feeling only slightly guilty at the manipulation. It was sinful really, but Devon was desperate for acceptance and had always looked up to Sam. But it was a means to an end.

All he'd have to do was avoid Sabine somehow so she didn't find out he was there, because if she did, she'd sure as shit have him thrown out immediately. No press was allowed. Luckily, Sabine only knew him as Sam Henderson and had no idea that he was actually Samuel Dove, sole heir to a multi-billion-dollar fortune, a fortune that he wanted very little to do with as long as his father expected him to take over the family business one day.

Sam was no stranger to going undercover. It wasn't like he'd never played up the rich-guy angle before to get intel he needed, and he'd definitely tapped into his endless resources and connections thanks to his family name, but tomorrow night he'd step into the role of suave, wealthy bachelor, not to get a story, but to get a few minutes alone with the sexy Lexi Monroe.

Okay…maybe also to get a story.

Chapter Two

Lexi had been holding back tears all night, but after a group hug with all the Kitty Cats, she'd barely made it to privacy before the torrent came. The party was supposed to be a celebration. Sabine had gone to a lot of trouble and expense to throw her the most extravagant retirement party, and here she was, once again hiding in a stall in the bathroom, trying to keep her tears from ruining her makeup.

Just like the interview the day before... Sabine had set up a meeting with the incomparable Sam Henderson, who was not only super hot but also screamed 'bad boy' to the extreme, which happened to be one of Lexi's major weak spots. Sabine had set it up to honor Lexi's career but Lexi had barely been able to speak to the man—not because he was hot, not because he was a bad boy, but because he hadn't had *that* look in his eyes. Lexi was so used to seeing the look of pity that everyone else seemed to have around her these days that he'd completely thrown her off by not looking at her like she was pathetic.

Sam hadn't seen her as a broken failure. No, Sam had been annoyed with her! He'd clearly been frustrated by her lack of candor and trying every trick he had, Lexi was sure, to get her to spill her secrets. So she'd done what she did best. She'd flirted with the man, turning on the heat so that he'd get so flustered that he wouldn't know what he wanted from her anymore. And it had worked so well that now she wasn't sure if she'd confused herself too.

She couldn't give him the details he so badly wanted, like secrets she kept for Sabine or information about the inner workings of the Kitty Cats, but she found him so enticing just because he had the audacity to treat her like she hadn't sustained a catastrophic injury that had destroyed her life. *The nerve of the man!* The way he'd looked at her…? Well, she was used to men ogling, but Sam had looked enthralled, like he'd appreciated her for the mystery that she was. She could tell that he'd wanted to peel her apart and strip her down, in more ways than one. And fuck, was that appealing.

But it was something she could never have. Sam was very much off limits for so many reasons. So, she was feeling sorry for herself, all caught up in the emotion of the night, thinking about things that only made her depression worse and sobbing away in the bathroom.

"Lexi, sweetie, you in here?" Vivian's voice echoed in the large marble room. "The speeches are about to start and Sabine's looking for you."

Lexi sighed. *Speeches, great.* "Yep, I'm here." She quickly wiped the last of her tears and flushed the toilet. When she opened the door, she was greeted by a concerned-looking Vivian.

"Oh honey, you need some touch-ups, stat." Vivian was the purchaser for all Cowan Enterprise's endeavors. From stocking the Kitty Cat Boutiques to making sure Sabine's various lines of kink wear and toys had the newest, most interesting products in existence, Vivian ran the show. She was a party planner for the company as well and had probably been the mastermind behind everything that was happening tonight. "Are you in pain? Have you got your meds?"

Another tear slipped past her eyelashes and tried for a smile. "I'm okay, Viv, seriously." She let the woman lead her to the mirror, where she got a good idea of how badly she needed to fix her makeup. She resembled a panda—or maybe a raccoon.

"We can get you a chair to sit in for the speeches, so you don't have to stand at the podium with everyone." Vivian was digging into her purse and pulling out all the necessities for a face-repair job.

"There's a podium?" Lexi squeaked.

Vivian looked up at her, her eyes wide. "Is that too much?" Her face crumbled into an expression of despair. "Oh, God, I didn't even think that it might be too much." She pulled Lexi into her arms and gave her a hug. "I'm sorry, honey. I—we—just wanted to give you a sendoff that was fitting. I'm so stupid for not realizing it would be overwhelming."

Before the accident, it wouldn't have been overwhelming. A party like this would have tickled Lexi like nothing else. She would have enjoyed every aspect of it and would have been partying into the wee hours of the morning. Since the accident, all she seemed to want to do was hide in her condo, only venturing out for Kitty Cat obligations that made it necessary to show her face. It was only her loyalty to Sabine that had kept her working for the last few months, but it had become clear that Lexi couldn't do it anymore. She'd lost whatever it was that had made her a successful Kitty

Cat before, and each Kitty Cat party she had forced herself to attend since had made her feel more miserable about everything she'd lost.

"No, Viv, the party is incredible, honestly. It's more than I deserve."

Viv pulled back enough to look sternly at Lexi. "Oh, girl, you deserve so much more. I wish you'd reconsider Sabine's offer. You could totally rock the trainer position—"

"No, I can't." The trainer role would have been something Lexi would have died to be offered…before the accident. Now it seemed like another one of those things that had been put out of her reach, like more gymnastics competitions, like continuing to coach the little ones who were only starting their gymnastics journeys. "I've got something in the works," she lied, forcing a smile onto her face. "It's all going to work out. I know it."

Vivian wasn't convinced, just like Sabine hadn't been either. Lexi picked up the tube of mascara from the counter before leaning in to assess the damage in the mirror. She needed to take care of the dark circles under her eyes.

As if reading her mind, Vivian passed her a tube of concealer. "How'd the interview go yesterday?"

Lexi cringed. "Not great."

"Was Sam too pushy?" Vivian's voice rose like she was ready to call Sam and personally give him shit. "I warned him—"

"Oh, no, he wasn't pushy." Lexi dabbed at the circles under her eyes. "I mean, he's a reporter, right? He wants a story."

"No matter the cost sometimes." Vivian sighed. "I know he's Sabine's friend, but sometimes I wonder why she keeps him around."

"Eye candy?" Lexi laughed. "You've gotta admit that he's not bad to look at."

Vivian put a finger on her jaw like she was contemplating. "Well, I wouldn't kick him out of my harem, if you know what I mean." She winked. "But he's a little rough around the edges, no?"

"Yeah, I guess." There was a ruggedness about Sam that rubbed Lexi in all the right ways. "I like that about him, though." And she hadn't been able get his sexy voice out of her head all day. It had been a nice distraction from the usual fretting as she lay awake in the wee hours.

"Hey, I'll forward you his number." Vivian was already on her phone before Lexi could protest that idea. "Maybe the two of you could hook up while he's in Miami."

Lexi's phone binged, presumably with Vivian's text. "I'm sure he's got better things to do." She picked up the mascara again and opened the top.

"Better than getting to know a sexy cat like you? Hardly. You two would make a cute couple, and I know Sam loves redheads."

Now that was news to Lexi. She wasn't going to lie. Her stomach did a flip.

"Give him a call. Adam mentioned that Sam didn't check out from the suite today, so he's still in Miami. Maybe he's got a story he's researching. You're here for the weekend too, right? Sounds like the perfect weekend romance setup to me."

Lexi nodded. That was the plan, a vacation courtesy of Sabine before starting her retirement for real. She'd intended to use the quiet time to figure out what the hell she was going to do with her life, but the closer that time got, the more daunting the task seemed.

"I don't know…maybe. Not sure I'm up for romance right now." Lexi wished she could suck back those words the second they left her mouth, because she saw the effect on Vivian instantly. Disappointment, followed by the usual…pity. Why couldn't Lexi be like she had been before the accident? Carefree…looking for an adventure? No one had said it to her, but Lexi could tell that they all wished she would put the accident behind her and get on with things.

The ensuing silence lasted for a couple of minutes. All the while, Lexi filled up with regret and remorse. Nothing seemed to be going smoothly ever since the accident. Nothing she said, nothing she did was right, and she really had no idea how to fix that.

Vivian ran her hand down Lexi's arm. "Hey, babe, you gotta do what you gotta do, but, Lexi?"

"Yeah?" Lexi didn't stop putting the mascara on, forcing herself to focus on fixing her makeup rather than looking at her friend and causing another blubbering mess of tears.

"You're a champion and we love you. The Kitty Cats won't be the same without you." Vivian brushed some hair back from Lexi's face. "I know for a fact that Sam would be totally into you, just like I know for a fact that there's no expiration date on Sabine's job offer. You've gotta put some faith in yourself, girl."

Lexi swallowed back the lump in her throat, nodded, then forced another smile on her face. "Sometimes you've gotta move on." And sometimes the pain from her back injury kept her up all night, despite the meds she was forced to take every day. And sometimes, when she did manage to fall asleep, it wasn't for more than an hour at a time, because she would wake up with such horrifying dreams, replaying the accident over and over again in her subconscious.

She was broken—damaged goods—and she needed to start fresh and figure out who she was going to be now that her identity had been shattered. She couldn't be a Kitty Cat. She didn't know how to be anymore. She couldn't be involved in a romance, not even a weekend one, because too much of her was cowering in the shadows, afraid to trust another person like she had before the accident.

"I know, hon. You're the strongest person I've ever met." Vivian offered her lip gloss with a smile. "You ready to go back out there and greet your adoring fans?"

Lexi felt the old, familiar spark of excitement at those words. She did have fans—many of them—and lots of friends too. Everyone who knew her, worked with her, even some clients, had come to bid her farewell, despite the fact that she was a fucking mess right now. It was special, and for someone who used to love attention, it touched her heart in ways she couldn't really deal with right now, hence the tears. "I'm ready." She finished dabbing on the lip gloss. "How do I look?"

"Stunning, as always." Vivian looped her arm into the crook of Lexi's elbow and tugged her toward the door, leaving her purse and makeup behind. "I'll grab that stuff later. Let's get you out there so you can hear Sabine's speech." Vivian leaned in closer. "She worked for days on it and wouldn't let Cammie edit it, so you better prepare yourself, 'cause it's gonna be a good one."

Lexi laughed. "Maybe I shouldn't have bothered fixing my makeup then."

Vivian winked as she opened the bathroom door. "If Sabine doesn't make you cry, she'll consider it a personal failure, I'm sure."

They both laughed, knowing that statement was the truth. Sabine was a perfectionist in everything she did. As much as Lexi was dreading the next hour, she secretly craved it too. Knowing that she was loved and hearing how much was something she knew would caress her battered soul. She hoped she'd be able to reflect on that love in the coming months as she grieved leaving the only family she'd ever felt truly accepted by.

* * * *

"Lexi, baby, we just heard about the sickest party going down later. You in?" Tanya, one of the newer Kitty Cats, came bounding toward Lexi like an overexcited kitten.

Lexi was sipping her mocktail, enjoying the party now that the speeches were over. She had cried, like a baby, but it was all good. The speeches had been heartfelt and had meant so much to her. She hadn't cared that her makeup had smeared in front of everyone. They'd been happy tears, mostly. "What party?"

Tanya nodded toward the corner where an entourage of people was milling about. "Devon Caldone is here." She leaned in to Lexi, lowering her voice so that no one around them would hear. "He's having a weekend party on his yacht and he wants some of the Kitty Cats to come. We told him that we can't do more than a night or so, but he's cool with that. He asked for you specifically."

Lexi's eyebrows shot up. Devon Caldone was an uber-wealthy socialite whose fame had everything to do with the gobs of money in his bank account and nothing to do with his winning personality. "Did he now?" He was the kind of guy who used his money to entice people but demanded a lot in return.

"Yeah, we're leaving soon, I think. He needs to talk to Sabine about something."

"Oh really?" Lexi sipped her drink and watched as Devon and his gaggle of followers moved closer to Sabine. She was talking to Senator Brunen, laughing, fully engaged and totally ignoring Devon as he approached. Lexi had no doubt that Sabine knew he was there, but Sabine thought the socialite was a nuisance and had told Lexi many times that the guy was no better than a gnat buzzing around her for attention—and he wanted her attention, badly. He'd secured himself invites to the Kitty Cat parties mainly because he was willing to pay the high cost of the most privileged membership to Sabine's Gentlemen's Club, and that came with all the invites all the time, so this wasn't the first time he'd attempted to get Sabine to talk to him.

"So, are you coming? I've heard his yacht is huge. There's even a pool on deck. I read an article once about the chef that he brings with him on all his cruises, some top-tier French guy. We've got to fly to New York on Saturday night, so you can leave with us if you want." Tanya tugged Lexi's hand and fluttered her eyelashes at her. "Come, Lexi. It'll be fun!"

Meh… Pre-accident Lexi would have been all over a yacht party, if only for the experience. "Nah, you girls go without me. I'm tired." Which was not a lie. "And my back hurts." Which kinda was a lie. It didn't hurt any more or less than it usually did, but it was the kind of excuse that easily got her out of most things.

"Oh, damn, I forgot all about that." Tanya winced. "You've been standing all night, you poor thing." She started to rub Lexi's back but must have thought better of it when Lexi flinched. "Do you need anything?"

"No, I'm good." She smiled warmly. Tanya meant well, as did most people who fussed whenever Lexi reminded them of her injury. "Standing actually hurts less than sitting." She laughed awkwardly. "And I've got my drink." She held up her mocktail and swished it around.

"Well, if you change your mind about the party, call me." Tanya winced again as they watched Devon attempt to involve himself in Sabine and the Senator's conversation.

There was an awkward pause, then Devon looked as though he was telling an animated joke. Of course, Sabine made quick work of him, cutting him down with a scathing look and a few short words. Devon's cheeks got ruddy and one of his followers yanked on his arm as if to extricate him from further social awkwardness.

"I think we'll be leaving sooner rather than later," Tanya said.

"Yeah, looks like Sabine just handed him his balls." Lexi loved Sabine. She was such a powerful woman, bowing to no man *ever*. Lexi turned back to Tanya. "Anyway, thanks for offering, but I think I'm going to head to the hotel and get some rest, sit this party out. Have a good time, though! I'm sure the yacht will be totally awesome."

Tanya gave her a quick hug. "Won't be the same without you, Lexi." Then she was gone, disappearing into the crowd within seconds.

"How you doin', lady?" Sabine sidled up next to Lexi and wrapped an arm around her waist. "Havin' a good time?"

Lexi nodded. "It's been a great night, thank you. I've had a wonderful time."

Sabine studied her for a few seconds and Lexi couldn't help but feel it like a penetrating stare. Sabine could read her like no one else. "You've been crying, though."

"Well, your speech…" Lexi tried for a laugh, but it came out like a croak.

"Before that. I saw you slip away. You okay? I can postpone my flight if you need me to stick around for a bit."

"Oh hell no!" Lexi put her now-empty glass on a passing waiter's tray. "You and Trent have been dying to have some time off." Sabine's partner, Trent Brooks, had planned the perfect getaway for him and Sabine — one that had been delayed so many times due to various situations that Lexi was sure it was costing a fortune to move the dates for flights and accommodations. "You need this vacation."

"I do," Sabine sighed. "We do." She smiled at Trent, who was motioning to his watch. Sabine turned away from him so she could face Lexi full-on. She put her hands on Lexi's arms and looked her right in the eyes. "But we can stick around for you if that's what you need right now."

"No, no." Lexi pulled Sabine in for a hug, feeling both grateful and undeserving all over again. "I'm fine! I'm going to enjoy the spa at the hotel and order all the room service I can. You'll see when you get the bill."

Sabine laughed and squeezed Lexi before letting her go. "You'd better!"

"I will." She smiled at Sabine, hoping that it came across as genuinely carefree. "I'm good. Promise. We'll have lunch when you get back to New York, and I'll fill you in on all my plans."

"I'm gonna hold you to that, lady." Sabine pointed at her. "Call Cammie if you need anything. Trent and I agreed to leave our phones off for the trip." She rolled her eyes. "Adam is going to visit Missy in Montana for a couple of months, but call him if something comes up. He has the private jet, so he can get to where you are in just a few hours."

"I will." *Not.* Adam only got to see his girlfriend a few months at a time because she was the sheriff of a little town in Montana, and Adam was still working as Sabine's head of security in New York. *Talk about a long-distance relationship.* They made it work, though, and there was no way Lexi would interrupt their precious time together.

"Promise?"

She hugged Sabine again. "Promise. Now go on your trip already! I can practically feel Trent's anxiety escalating by the minute."

Sabine glanced over her shoulder. "Yeah, he looks about ready to blow. Okay." She turned back to Lexi. "Take care, and we'll see you in a few weeks."

"Absolutely! Have a wonderful trip and take lots of pictures!"

Sabine was already on the move, waving over her shoulder as she beelined for her lover, Trent.

Lexi sighed. She aspired to one day find a love like that for herself. Then she sighed again, because really, who was she kidding? Love like that only happened to unbroken people, and Lexi was a shattered mess with way too many dark secrets that she wasn't willing to share with anyone.

Chapter Three

It took Lexi a while to say all the goodbyes. She made her rounds, sucked back her sorrow and was headed out of the back door when she remembered she'd left her purse in the pantry. Her mind was definitely on other things. She peeked through the door of the main hall and cringed at the thought of running the gauntlet of goodbyes again. The banquet hall they'd rented for the party had to have a separate entrance to the kitchen. It was just a matter of finding it.

Lexi snuck down the back corridor that curved around the main dining room and opened a few doors before finding one that would take her through to the kitchen. She ducked into the pantry, bypassing the staff who were still pumping out food for all the guests, and found her purse in a pile of others belonging to the Kitty Cats. Her hotel key card, phone, money and ID, as well as her ever-important pain meds, were tucked inside. No way she could do without any of that for the night.

She pulled out her phone and texted Carlo, her driver, to let him know that she was ready to leave and for him to meet her out back, then she slipped into the corridor that, she was thankful, no one seemed to know about. There were so many doors that she hadn't opened, and she was a tiny bit curious about what lay behind them all. The banquet hall itself was a doozy, with twenty-five dining halls alone, and sat right on the beach. It was a popular location for many extravagant weddings and was well-known for its grandeur as well as its catering. Sabine had spared no expense for Lexi's retirement bash. Normally Lexi would have indulged with the rest of the Kitty Cats, found herself a man she thought appealing and had a party of her own back at her hotel room, but those days seemed long past, and all Lexi could think about now was sinking into her bed and putting her once-beloved world behind her. *Sometimes it's better to move on.* Words she said so often she had to wonder if she was trying to convince herself as much as she was attempting to persuade everyone else.

"I don't care what you think. I don't pay you to think!"

Lexi heard the angry voice behind a closed door, even though whoever was talking was clearly trying to keep their volume low. Totally *failing* at keeping his voice down, too.

"No, I didn't get a chance to talk to Sabine. She was surrounded by people all night, then she disappeared early. She's on some vacation or something."

Lexi was going to keep walking until she heard Sabine's name. She stopped right outside the door where the voice, which she suddenly recognized as Devon Caldone's, was coming from, and felt no shame at eavesdropping. If he was talking about Sabine, it was Lexi's business to listen.

"Fuck, don't you think I know that? I've been trying to talk to that bitch for the last six months and she keeps blowing me off."

Lexi moved closer to the door and practically pressed her ear against it.

"Yeah, well, I've got some of her Kitty Cats coming onto the yacht. Trust me. I'll get the info I need, then we can move on Cowan Enterprises. She's not going to know what hit her." There was a pause, a long pause, and Lexi thought for a second that he was going to come to the door, but then his voice rose again, and he sounded farther away. "Do you know who you're talking to? I'm not scared of Vince or his crew." Another pause. "Well, you may think that, but it's not what's going to happen. I'll get the info, then Sabine Cowan will be nothing more than a slut with an empty bank account."

Lexi had heard enough. She lifted her phone and started quickly walking away from the door, her eyes on her contacts. Who should she call? Sabine? With what information? That Devon Caldone was making vague threats against her? It wasn't like Sabine hadn't faced that kind of thing before. And Lexi didn't want to disturb her on her vacation. Even though Sabine said she was leaving her phone off, that was highly unlikely for such a type-A person. But still, Lexi didn't know enough to bother her and Trent.

There was Adam, but he was likely already in Montana, focused on his sheriff girlfriend, and again, she didn't really have anything to tell him. He did security checks on every member of the Kitty Cat Gentlemen's Club, so he would know everything there was to know about Devon Caldone. Adam was always thorough.

No, Lexi had to get more information before she would bother anyone about this, whatever it was. Devon Caldone could be blowing hot air and needing to lick his wounded pride because of how Sabine had brushed him off earlier. Lexi was trained to do this kind of recon anyway, and she was good at it. *Had* been good at it—before the accident, at least. The last few months she'd mostly been incapable of getting out of her own head. But she had an invite to the yacht party, so she could get herself onto that boat. She'd have to figure out the rest once she was there. She wasn't worried about the other Kitty Cats spilling any information, but all the same, she wanted to be there to figure out what the hell Devon was after. She'd have to get hold of Tanya to let her know she was going to come on the yacht after all.

She was rounding the corner, her eyes still on her phone, scrolling for Tanya's number, when she stepped right into someone's burly body.

"*Oof!*" She would have bounced back and probably fallen straight onto her ass if the owner of the burly body hadn't encircled her waist with his big arms...his big, heavily tattooed arms... She'd seen that ink before. "Sam?"

Sam's long hair was down, parted to the side and looking glossy, soft and darker than it had when it had been put up. He was wearing a dark blue shirt with a few buttons undone that showcased his muscular chest, which was also covered in tattoos.

"Whoa there." Sam's gruff-sounding chuckle sent a shiver of pure, unexpectedly intense lust up Lexi's spine. "I wasn't expecting anyone to be back here."

"Sam?" Lexi felt like her brain had been rattled out of whack. "What are you doing here?" Reporters were not allowed at any Kitty Cat function.

"Yo, Samuel, we're out of here." Devon breezed past Lexi, stopping to pat Sam on the back and cock an eyebrow as he shifted his gaze from Sam to Lexi. "Looks like you caught the girl of the hour." He flashed a grin. "You're planning on coming to the after-party on my boat, right? I've got a couple of limos out back. Would love to have such an honored guest aboard."

"Uh, I—"

"She's coming." Sam tightened his hold on her waist, pulling her to his side. "She's with me."

"Oh yeah? Nice catch, bro!" Devon whacked Sam on the back one more time. "We'll see you in the car."

"We'll meet you at the boat. Lexi needs to grab some stuff from her hotel." Sam nodded down at her like she knew what the fuck was going on.

Luckily, her head bobbed in agreement without her mind having to think too hard on it.

"Great, we'll see you there. Boat leaves at one, so don't be late. We're going to party until the sun comes up!" Devon kept walking, making it to the end of the hall and out of sight in seconds.

"What happened?" Lexi didn't know if she should say anything to Sam about what she'd overheard.

"Devon is up to something." Sam glanced quickly over his shoulder. "And I'm going to find out what it is."

Lexi opened her mouth, then closed it. What could she say? What did she actually know? She had too many questions running through her mind and they were getting all jumbled up.

"I need you on that boat with me." Sam loosened his hold on her waist.

She wanted to ask why, but her mind jumped to the reality that she needed to be on that boat too. She had find out what information Devon was after and how he was planning on bankrupting Sabine. "I heard him saying something about Sabine," she admitted.

"Yeah, he's been mumbling shit all night about her. I wasn't planning on spending the weekend with the guy, but something's going on and my gut is telling me it's something juicy."

"Is that why you're here? Are you on assignment?"

"No. Not officially, anyway." He folded her arm around his and started walking, forcing her to keep up. "I assumed you needed stuff from your hotel for the weekend."

"I do, I guess." She stopped, digging in her heels to keep them from heading out the back door. "Sam, seriously, why *are* you here? You know Sabine doesn't let—"

His expression darkened and he gave her a once-over that was full of heat and stopped her next words from tumbling out. Then he pushed her back until her body pressed up against the wall. With his arms caging her, his hands bracing beside her head, he leaned in, and she was sure she was about to spontaneously combust. She inhaled his scent—vanilla, clove and something spicy—and her body melted even more. "I'm here for you, Lexi, and I don't care if Sabine would approve."

She gulped. His eyes were so blue, his hair cascaded around his face and his beard was almost touching her. She licked her lips. "You're here for me?" It sounded possessive and a little dangerous. Her skin felt like it was rippling with pent-up excitement.

"I can't stop thinking about you." He was breathing hard, his chest rising and falling, almost brushing against her tits. She wanted him to touch her. She wanted it so badly that she could have screamed.

"You can't?"

He shook his head once, his gaze travelling to her lips. "Nope."

She shifted closer, lifting her hand so she could touch the side of his face then trail along the length of his beard. It was softer than she'd expected. He shivered at her touch, his eyes closing briefly. When he opened them again, the intensity of his stare startled her. "You in or what?"

Lexi gulped. Nodded.

She was expecting him to push away, to tug her arm and keep walking, but instead, he leaned closer and his beard brushed against her cheek as he lowered his lips to hers. He moved one hand to her ass, hauling her up so that she was pressed against his body. She felt his hard cock against her stomach. He moved his other hand to her face, cupping her cheek as he brushed his lips gently against hers. "When we're with Devon, you call me Samuel, understand?"

Lexi made a noise that she hoped sounded like 'yes'.

"And I expect you to keep everything you learn about me confidential, even from Sabine." He brushed her lips again, sending a shiver of anticipation straight through her body. "You're good at keeping secrets, aren't you, Lexi?" He moved his hand to the back of her neck then tilted her head up.

She wanted to blurt out, 'not from Sabine!' but she was locked in with his intense eyes. Her body was melting away and she wanted so badly for him to really kiss her. She wanted a taste of him.

"There are things about me that Sabine doesn't know." His voice was deliciously gruff. Lexi could listen to him speak all night and day. "And I want to keep it that way."

"Okay," Lexi croaked. *Wait… What am I agreeing to?*

He nodded, his grip on her ass tightened, then finally, he lowered his mouth to hers and kissed her like he should have ten minutes before. He stroked her tongue and nipped her bottom lip, devouring her so that he took her breath away and she had to fight with everything she had not to rub herself all over him. She wanted to slide down his body and take his cock into her mouth. She wanted to feel his weight pressing down onto her as he pumped her full of his cum.

She wanted Sam Henderson, and she hadn't wanted anyone this badly in a very long time.

When he broke away, it was on an explosion of breath and he was panting like she was. "We may never get out of this hallway." He pressed his forehead to hers. "You in this with me, Lexi? Like all in?"

For the first time since her accident, Lexi felt alive with hope. Her body was tingling with pleasure instead of the usual pain. "I'm all in," she said, without thinking too much about it.

Sam pulled back a bit so he could run his thumb over her cheek, her jaw then across her bottom lip. "Then you need to know that my name is Samuel Dove, and my family is into every black-market deal there is."

Lexi's mouth fell open. She knew who the Dove family was. Really, who didn't? They were notorious for over-the-top displays of wealth and extravagance. Their money was rumored to be in the billions. They were a crime family that had somehow managed to capture the spotlight and reach celebrity status for being corrupt and terrifying in a loveable kind of way. That was probably thanks to the reality show that had run years before, featuring the family in all their glory.

She had never watched it, but her parents had. Now she was curious to find out if Sam had been on the show too. Somehow, she doubted it. He didn't seem like the reality show kind of guy. From what she remembered hearing about the TV series, the family was all about the flash, bang and theatrics. Sam didn't have that vibe at all. He was chill and low-key all the way, which Lexi found very attractive. She needed a little chill in her life.

In any case, what Lexi believed was that the FBI wanted the Dove family something fierce. The DEA watched them like hawks. There were stories about them floating around for every horrible thing a person could ever think of where crime families were concerned—extortion, kidnapping, even murder—and there were some rumors that they had personal access to the President himself. They were not a family anyone wanted to mess around with or even glance at the wrong way…if any of that were true, anyway. Somehow, looking at Sam now, she had her doubts that he'd come from a family that was half that bad. The Dove family spent a lot of time in the tabloids, so who knew what was actual fact or fiction?

Sam rubbed her cheek again. "But don't worry, Lexi. My family isn't a part of my life."

Is that a good or bad thing?

"At least, I don't want them to be part of my life, hence the alias, Sam Henderson."

"Okay." She had so many questions rolling through her head. *How did he manage to leave his family? Why did he leave his family? Do they know he's a reporter?*

"But Devon knows me as Samuel Dove, and I need him to think I can help him get whatever it is he wants so that I can get a story out of this."

Lexi forced herself to speak. "I need to know what he's up to, if it involves Sabine."

Sam nodded once, his eyes still very penetrating and intense. "Then we're in this together."

It wasn't a question, but Lexi nodded all the same. "We're in this together."

"Let's go to your room."

Lexi knew he meant to get her things, but her body badly wanted it to mean so much more. She let him lead her to the back door, and for the first time in a long time, Lexi was ready for whatever lay ahead.

Chapter Four

"Let me take the lead." Sam wanted to ravish Lexi, so when he said that, he meant both in the investigation as well as in bed. And they *would* end up in bed together. Sam was sure of that.

As if reading his mind, Lexi's cheeks took on a pink hue that not only made her freckles pop but also shocked the shit out of him. For a Kitty Cat of her caliber to blush…well, he must be doing something right.

Fuck, he wanted to lick every single freckle on her body.

"That's how I usually roll." Her voice was sultry satin that made his cock harden and his balls tighten. She looked up at him through her eyelashes and bit her bottom lip.

"Remember who I am." He pulled her close to his side as they walked up the gangway to the yacht. She fit so perfectly against him that he could lean down and kiss the top of her head if he wanted.

"I wouldn't dare forget." She reached her hand out as Devon approached. "Hi, I'm Lexi Monroe. We haven't met properly."

"So formal!" Devon laughed, his arms open as if he was going to pull Lexi away for a hug.

Sam felt her stiffen against his side, which gave his ego a great stroke and also gave him a clear signal that he needed to put a quick stop to this. "Hands off, bud. This one's mine."

Devon barked out a laugh. "So possessive." He raised his hands. "Okay, man, okay, I won't touch your girl." He winked at Lexi. "But maybe later she could put on a show for us. I've got some satin ribbons hanging from the ceiling in the lounge especially for you."

Lexi was still all tensed up. "Uh, you do? Oh, well, maybe I can—"

Oh hell no! From what he'd gathered during their interview yesterday, even without a lot of details about her injury, he knew Lexi wasn't going to be doing any ribbon acrobatics any time soon. "You know I don't like to share my women, Devon. She's for my eyes only." Sam could do the dominant alpha thing, but he knew he was laying it on pretty thick. Sadly, it was the only sure way to get Devon to back off. Being obnoxious was a language Devon spoke well.

Much to Sam's relief, Lexi relaxed into him, like she was okay with what he was saying.

"Whoa, dude, all right, all right." Devon attempted to laugh Sam's aggression off, but Sam could tell that he was rubbing his host the wrong way. Devon didn't much like being told no. He leaned in closer. "You talk to your family yet?"

"I'm working on it," Sam said, enough of an answer to get Devon smiling again but not enough to commit to anything Sam couldn't deliver on. The truth was that Sam had no intention of connecting Devon to anyone in his family for any reason—but especially not his father. They'd mix like they were meant to be together, and that might give his father dastardly ideas that would make him more of a criminal than he already was. In fact, Devon would have fit better into the Dove clan than Sam ever had. Sam knew for sure that Devon would have jumped at the chance to be on the reality show when it had been airing, unlike Sam, who had avoided the filming as much as the family's contract had allowed.

"Good man." Devon whacked him on the back before pointing to the left. "My people will make sure your stuff gets to your room. The party is only getting started. Come, my sexy friends. Let's get you some booze!"

* * * *

Sam hadn't been able to get it out of his head that, by some twist of fortune, he and Lexi were going to be sharing a room very soon—possibly a bed too. He'd been fixated on that reality and the fulfillment of his fantasy of being intimately close to her ever since they'd stepped foot on the yacht. If he had his way, he'd have taken her to bed hours before. Hell, he'd have taken her against the wall, in the shower, on the floor… Whatever she wanted would have been good with him.

But Devon was in full-on party mode, which could go on for hours still, especially because of whatever the man was snorting. There was no way Sam would get anything useful out of the guy when he was in host mode and high as fuck, but he couldn't leave quite yet either, because Devon would get pissy if he felt like he was being snubbed.

Lexi was on the other side of the room, chatting with her Kitty Cats. She'd spent time mingling, introducing herself, being vivacious, just like Sam knew her to be in all her promo material that he'd researched. This Lexi was vastly different from the woman he'd interviewed the morning before. Sam didn't know her well, but he had watched her for the last couple of hours, and as much as she was exuding party vibes to everyone near her, to Sam she showed signs of distress. There were dark circles under her eyes, and he'd caught her bracing her hand on her lower back a few times, like she was keeping herself from falling over or perhaps trying to manage pain. He knew the injuries she'd sustained over a year ago had been significant, but he'd never been able to find many details. That was strange, considering how media-friendly every other part of her gymnastics career had been.

The most telling sign that she was done for the night was when she looked away, thinking no one was watching. She bit her lip, not in the sexy way she'd done with Sam. No, this was a bite that came with a pained look on her face, and she looked like she was trying to stop herself from crying.

"Samuel, what's with the dirty beard look?" Devon reached over and swatted at the bottom of Sam's beard. "You auditioning for the role of a hobo or something?" He turned his attention to the crowd. "Did you know that Samuel's family was a Friday night reality show special for five years? It was before most of your times, but I bet you can still find episodes online."

All eyes turned back to Sam.

He swallowed a growl, electing to play nice, even though Devon was pushing his buttons. "My father acquired the rights to the show years ago." And as far as Sam knew, there were no episodes available for streaming or downloading. He didn't know if his father was planning on re-releasing the seasons at some time, but he hoped not.

"Samuel's in a few episodes and you'd never recognize him." Devon made to swat Sam's beard again, but Sam shifted away. "Totally clean cut, pretty boy, eh, Samuel? Now you look like an honest-to-God thug." He lifted his hands. "No offense, man. Seriously, it's a good look on you. Very rugged."

Sam gulped down half his beer. He needed this night to end already before he did something to Devon that he'd regret in the morning.

"How much is your family worth?" Devon had always asked questions like that when they were back in school and apparently it hadn't changed. It was some kind of dick-measuring contest he was determined to win. "A few billion by now? I heard your dad acquired that film company in Germany. What's it called?"

"Fetish Films." Sam took a swig of his beer while he kept Lexi in his sights. She was touching her back again, and this time she was grinding her fist along the side of her spine.

"Yeah, that's it. They make pretty hard-core porn. You have access to the sets at all? Maybe you could get us in for a tour." He didn't wait for Sam to answer. "Samuel's family is totally connected in all the right ways. Last I heard, the family's net worth was two-point-five billion."

His buddies laughed and the girls who were draped all over Devon gasped.

"I think it's more along the lines of four billion now." Sam finished his beer and put it on the coffee table.

Devon whistled. "Ladies, this would have been the most eligible wealthy bachelor in the room but..." Devon pointed toward Lexi, who was making her way over to them. She still had on her three-inch heels, and Sam could tell that the sultry movement of her hips was not a show she was putting on for their benefit. It was exhaustion making her sway.

As she moved into range, Sam stood, and in one quick movement, swooped her up into his arms. "Time to take my lady to bed." He nuzzled her neck and whispered, "Is this okay? Am I hurting you?"

She draped her arm around his neck. "My knight in shining armor."

Everyone laughed, Devon made a lewd comment, but the look Lexi was giving Sam screamed relief and peace and let him know that he really was helping her. She had a death grip on his neck, though, so he also knew she was still struggling with the pain.

"You!" Devon snapped his fingers at one of the staff members who was carrying a plate of appetizers toward the main table. "Show Mr. Dove and Ms. Monroe to their room."

Much to her credit, the woman Devon barked at didn't react other than to nod, put the tray down then motion to Sam so he would follow.

As soon as he turned toward the door, Lexi put her head on his chest and curled her body into his. "Thank you," she whispered. Then she opened her purse and slipped her hand inside. She pulled out a pill that looked like a prescription and popped it into her mouth.

He had to assume she was on painkillers, especially if her injury—whatever it entailed—had involved her back. "You okay?"

"I will be." She sighed. "I don't like taking my meds. They make my head feel like it's filled with cotton balls."

"Hard to concentrate?"

"Yeah. Can't follow conversations well."

"They put you to sleep?"

"Not anymore." She ran her fingers up the back of his neck, sending shivers of pleasure straight down his spine. "But they do take the edge off."

The woman walking ahead stopped at a set of double doors. "Mr. Caldone's suite is at the end of the hall. You and he have the only rooms on this level." She said it like Sam should be impressed…or grateful. When he didn't react, she opened the door and stepped back. "If you need anything, just pick up the phone. It dials straight to the galley."

"Thank you," Sam grunted.

Their cabin was luxurious and definitely had to be one of the bigger rooms on the yacht, aside from Devon's. He'd always pandered to Sam, making sure Sam had the best of everything whenever they'd hung out back in their college days. At that time, Sam had still been living with the lies that his family had constantly manufactured for the benefit of their many misinformed fans. Part of his family's fame had come from the reality TV show that had filmed at one of their estates, and because of that, they'd had an image to uphold that, at times, hadn't really fit with the reality of being a crime family. While a lot of what had been filmed was an accurate representation of them — the constant yelling, the threatening posturing toward this enemy or that, the backdoor deals and clandestine meetings — the producers had hyped some things up while ignoring others, all in an effort to make the Dove family safe for prime-time TV. Devon had been right. Sam had been in a few episodes, which made him all the more desirable as a friend or a fuck back at his college. Devon had certainly wanted to be with him all hours of the day and night.

Sam had lived like a rich frat boy, partying all night and barely functioning in class all day, and Devon had been there the whole time, making sure Sam always had the best drugs, the best booze, the best girls. It seemed as though things hadn't changed much in the time since he'd seen Devon last.

Sam's family was powerful. The Dove name opened a lot of doors...corrupt, morally deranged doors, but still, it got Sam things — and right now, Sam had no problem milking that for what it was worth. Devon was a sneaky fuck at the best of times, but Sam knew enough already to suggest that Devon was dabbling in things that were way over his head. He would have brushed it off as bragging, but Devon had let a few things slip earlier in the evening that had piqued Sam's curiosity and pinged his instincts for a good story.

"Wow, this is nicer than the suite Sabine put me in." Lexi, still in his arms, was scanning as much as she could see of the cabin. "I don't think I've ever seen so much gold used as decoration before."

"Devon likes his bling." Sam laid her gently on the bed. "You look like you're ready to pass out. Rest. I'm going to do a bit of snooping while Devon's busy with his guests."

Lexi grabbed onto his shirt and pulled him back down. "No, don't go." She took a breath, her eyes wide and locked into his. "I need—" She hesitated, swallowed. "I need—"

He knew she was in pain and that she was exhausted. This close up, it was impossible not to see that written on her face, but there was something else there too...desire, want. *Lust.* His cock was hard already. He licked his lips. "What do you need, Lexi?"

"I need to feel normal." Tears welled in her eyes. "Kiss me," she breathed.

It was impossible not to oblige. He leaned in and pressed his mouth to hers, prodding her lips open so he could slip inside. She tasted like cherries. *So sweet.* Her lips were soft cushions that he so badly wanted wrapped around his dick.

She tore herself away and nailed him with a look filled with all kinds of demands. "Kiss me hard. Don't treat me like I'm going to break."

Then he knew. Everyone must have been walking on eggshells around Lexi since her accident, treating her like a porcelain doll, when in reality she was hardly that delicate. She needed something from him, and it wasn't tenderness—not right now, at least. She was speaking a language of pain that he intimately understood.

"On your knees," he said sternly.

Her eyes sparked and a slow grin spread on her pretty lips. She moved to the side of the bed and rose onto her knees. He grabbed the back of her neck, pulling her closer so that her tits brushed against his chest. His cock throbbed for her and he could think of a million ways he wanted to take her body. But right now, what she needed was a proper kiss, and he knew just how to make her toes curl.

With brutal force, he kissed her again, pushing past the gate of her mouth, putting everything he had into making sure she felt him. She swayed closer and put her hands over his shoulders, then pressed herself against him. She was making little whimpering noises that let him know he was doing right by her. Her licked her, sucked her, even nipped at her sexy bottom lip before diving back inside to stroke her tongue and entangle himself with her. He could eat this woman alive. He wanted to taste every part of her.

When he pulled back, she let out a gasp, her eyes half-closed. He put pressure on her neck, so she got the idea and slid down his body. With her ass in the air, she worked his belt then his pants. His dick was throbbing, weeping pre-cum for her mouth. From the moment he'd first watched Lexi dancing in one of her promotional videos, he'd wanted her. His brief interactions with her over the years had only whet his appetite until now, when she was making herself completely available to him. He could hardly contain his lust. He wanted to ravish her, to strip her bare and fuck her hard. But he also wanted to savor every second he had with her, because he wasn't stupid enough to think a girl like Lexi would want to stay with a guy like him after this weekend.

As soon as his cock was free from his pants, she had it in her warm hands and she was watching him as she stroked gently down his length then back up again. "Don't be gentle," he growled. "It's not gonna break."

She laughed, a throaty, sexy sound, and it was the best thing he'd heard all night. She teased him with a kiss to the tip of his cock that made him jolt, made him twist his fist into her hair. Fuck, this woman was going to shatter him. He wanted her—all of her. No matter what happened, when this weekend was over, he knew he was going to have a hard time letting her go.

She licked him from the tip of his cock all the way down to his balls, and his legs almost gave way. When she sucked his sac into her hot, wet mouth, he knew he could die right then and be happy.

But Lexi seemed to be just getting started.

Chapter Five

She took him all the way back to the wall of her throat then did something with her jaw and swallowed him whole, every fucking inch, right down to the hilt. *Holy fuck!* With her tongue pressing against his shaft and a vibrating purr coming from her, he felt ten million sensations at once, all centered on his cock. She palmed his balls, using just enough pressure into it to send jolts of pure ecstasy through his body. He groaned when she started to pull back, stroking, flicking, licking her way to his tip. She repeated the cycle, taking him in, sucking him off, kneading his balls and overall making it impossible not to spew his load down her throat, which he did, bellowing his way through the most explosive orgasm he'd had in a long time.

He was panting, his head spinning, but he wasn't too out of it not to give her back what she'd given him. "Strip. I want you naked. *Now.*" His voice was a raw bark of sound that he barely recognized. It'd been a while since he'd had such an amazing blow job.

Actually, it might have been *never* since he'd had one quite like that.

Lexi dabbed the corner of her lips with her tongue, catching a bit of cum that was still there. It was so hot that his cock was instantly hard once again. But that was nothing compared to the strip tease she gave him. It wasn't just watching her slowly slide each piece of clothing off her glorious body. It was the look in her eyes, like she wanted him to see her, *really* see her. She wanted to strip herself bare and expose herself in every way. It might have been wishful thinking on his part, because he wanted so badly to get into that beautiful head of hers along with her body, but he sure as shit hoped not.

She was all muscles and power. Her stomach was ribbed with abs, and her skin looked so soft and smooth that he couldn't wait to run his tongue along every curve and crevice. Her tits were small and perky, freckled like the rest of her body, suggesting that she'd been sun-kissed there many times. Her nipples — small, pink and hard — were begging to be sucked, licked and nibbled on. His mouth was actually watering as he watched her finally slip her panties off to reveal a tiny strip of red curls, a shock of color against her pale skin. *So fucking hot.* He licked his lips.

"On your back, spread your legs."

She nodded, her eyes locked on his as she lowered herself back. Her hair cascaded across the pillows as she threw her arms haphazardly above her head, looking for all intents and purposes like a goddess waiting to be worshipped. She opened her legs, showing him her wet, pink pussy lips.

It took him less than five seconds to rip his own clothes off then climb onto the bed. He crawled over her, prodding her skin with his dick as he kissed his way up her body, along her ribs, to her tits and finally to her luscious lips. "You're so beautiful, Lexi."

She held the sides of his face and caressed his beard with her thumbs. "So are you."

He kissed her, took her mouth like he wanted to take her pussy, stroking her softly at first as he ran one hand down her body, tracing every curve and cut of her muscles. When he reached her pussy and slipped along her wet folds, he deepened their kiss, pummeling her mouth harder, faster, as he dipped his fingers inside her, pumping her mouth just like he was finger-fucking her sweet cunt.

She made pretty little noises deep in her throat that sounded like a purr, and as much as he would love to make her come right now, he also wanted to taste her pussy and lick her to climax. He reluctantly pulled away, breaking their kiss, trailing his fingers up her stomach as he moved down her body, kissing his way to his prize.

He spent some time on her tits, sucking each nipple into his mouth so he could roll those sweet buds between his teeth, making Lexi cry out, "Yes!" when he bit down on each in turn. Then he licked away the pinch, soothed the pain he'd inflicted and started all over again until she was writhing, her hips moving like she in agony, waiting for his attention down below.

Another day he might have denied her, made her wait, but he didn't have it in him tonight. He wanted this. He *needed* this. So he gave up her delicious tits and continued down, circling her belly button with his tongue, making her squirm until he got to those tight, soft little curls above her clit. The smell of her pussy made his mouth water, and her spicy heat made him moan. He licked his way down to her slit and sucked back her juice. He wanted to bury himself there, coat himself in her aroma and savor every taste he took.

When he latched on to her clit, she bucked her hips and cried out, urging him to give her what she needed. She played with her nipples, pinching, flicking, rubbing herself while he stroked her clit, pressing his tongue to her hard nub before sucking it into his mouth so he could roll his tongue over it again and again. She arched her back, and he licked harder until her pussy was quivering and her legs shaking. She moaned, gasping and panting through her orgasm. Her whole body shuddered until finally she collapsed, her arms back over her head. With her legs splayed and her eyes hooded, she looked all sexy, exhausted and satiated.

He moved up her body, crawling over her until he could kiss her lips and run his fingers through her hair. "You need sleep."

"Thank you, Sam," she whispered, her eyes sliding closed. "I needed that."

He brushed some hair from her cheek and traced his fingers down the side of her face. "I did too — more than you could know." But he knew she couldn't hear him because her breathing was deep and her eyelids fluttering like she was already dreaming of doing it with him again.

He kissed her gently then moved off the bed. He couldn't help gawking at her beautiful body as he dragged his clothes back on. She was a goddess, so exceptionally gorgeous that he could stare at her all day. She sighed, turned onto her side, and Sam saw what he assumed was the damage from her accident. His stomach clenched and he had an impulse to climb into bed and wrap her in his arms. Her scar was bubbled and purple and it ran down one side of her spine, about six inches in length. He didn't know if it was a surgery scar or from the actual accident, but he knew it was what caused her pain. Right there was where she had been rubbing when he'd caught sight of her at the party. She must have been in a world of pain when it had happened, with long-term residual pain impacting her daily life now.

A flash of possessive caveman shit whipped through him. He wanted to protect her, to shield her from more damage or further injury. He wanted to keep her safe — and he barely knew the woman. With a sigh, he pulled the covers over her and tore himself away.

She didn't need that macho-man crap from him. She needed someone who would treat her like a normal woman and not tiptoe around her injury. If he wanted her in his life in any capacity, even if it was only for the weekend, then he'd better bench the urge to baby her and embrace what she wanted. And he was certain that what she wanted was a Dom who would treat her right and make her moan — and that meant giving her some pain with her pleasure. He had a strong feeling that it was what she really needed most of all.

He knew first-hand what that was like. His tattoos were testament to his need for pain. It was his therapy of choice when he was in the depths of depression and his meds weren't cutting it. He'd tried the conventional route, even talked to a therapist at one point, but he'd quit that method of self-care quickly when he'd realized that he'd need to dig into some heavy issues related to his father that he was so not interested in exploring with a shrink. Maybe he'd given up on it too quickly, but he'd found other ways to cope. The pain he got from his tattoo artist was a comfort, a known entity and took all the bad shit he was feeling and brought it to the surface. It gave him an outlet, and the endorphins that followed weren't too bad either. It might seem fucked up to people who didn't know, but pain was sometimes the best medicine for pain. When a person controlled it, it became less oppressive.

He could do right by Lexi, give her what she wanted and, at least for the next couple of days, give her the release she needed.

Sam found his duffel bag in the walk-in closet and searched the secret pocket for his tools. He always came prepared when he was investigating, in case he had an opportunity to get some dirt.

If he knew Devon, the guy would still be partying on deck, even though the sun was starting to lighten the sky outside the cabin window. Sam grabbed his phone and slipped quietly out of the room.

No one was in the hall, but given that they were on a private floor of the yacht, he wouldn't expect there to be. He moved to the double doors of Devon's main suite then pressed his ear to it. There were no noises whatsoever. He pushed down on the door handle and was surprised when the latch clicked. He wouldn't need his pick kit after all, not for this door anyway. Sam poked his head in. The suite opened with a sitting room, complete with a black leather wraparound couch that looked like a bunch of reclining chairs stuck together, and a seventy-inch TV mounted on the wall. He moved in and shut the door behind him. There were no signs of partying happening here. Everything was immaculate. There were two doors along the back wall, both closed. Sam walked to the one on the right, which turned out to be a large bathroom. It was all marble and steel and had another door leading to the bedroom.

Sam walked through, once again closing the door behind him.

The bedroom was double the size of the one he and Lexi shared, but again, showed no signs of occupancy. Devon had not yet left the upper deck, but Sam knew that time was definitely running out. He opened the walk-in closet and did a quick search. Devon's closet was packed with designer clothes for every occasion. The man could be on the yacht for months without having to wear the same outfit twice. There were stacks of boots and shoes of all kinds too. It was a fortune in clothing alone. Sam rooted through it all, trying to be careful so he didn't disturb anything too much. He found a safe bolted to the floor that was open and empty.

He moved back into the main bedroom and rifled through the desk. There was a laptop stashed in one of the drawers, which he pulled out and booted up. It required thumbprint access, so that was a no-go. He put it back into the drawer so Devon wouldn't get suspicious. Sam scanned the room one more time.

The guy had nothing lying around to incriminate him, which was not surprising. Devon wasn't stupid. He was just an asshole. Sam couldn't plant a listening device, not only because ethically that would be getting into territory that he didn't want to cross *yet*, but also because in the state of Florida all parties needed to consent to a recording. They were only just off the coast of Miami, so maybe if they entered international waters then Sam could possibly cross that line, but it was something he'd have to be desperate enough to do — and right now he wasn't.

He was about to walk through the bedroom door to the living room area when he heard the main door open and Devon's booming voice soon follow.

"Yeah, man, I told you. She's on the boat. Got her in the suite next to mine. She's one of Sabine's main girls, high ranking, inner circle and all that." Devon's voice got closer, so Sam beat it back to the bathroom and slipped inside just as his host burst into the bedroom. "I'll get the information I need. Don't worry about that. She's a sweet thing, kinda stupid too. Won't be hard to get what I want."

Sam had kept the door open slightly so he could hear better, and bristled at Devon's comments. Lexi wasn't stupid, and Sam doubted very much that she'd be easily manipulated. All the same, Sam needed to give her a heads-up so she knew what was coming.

Devon collapsed onto the bed and let out a loud groan. "Nah, my man is solid. Samuel's gonna hook us up with his family soon, then we'll have another way to get that Cowan bitch. His dad is moving in on the sex industry overseas in direct competition with her. He'll be interested."

Oh yeah, Devon had that right. Sam's dad would be interested in cornering the smut market in the US. *My father will never find out about it, though.*

"Dude, I need to get some sleep. Fuck off, would ya?" The bed squeaked. "Hey, you know I'm joking. I didn't mean any offense, for fuck's sake." He paused again. "Right, got it. Listen... I've got some sexy Kitty Cat girls on the way, and I need to take a shower. I'll call you tonight."

Sam had to get the hell out of the bathroom. He moved to the other door and quickly stepped into the living area, shutting the door as Devon went into the bathroom.

There was a quick knock on the main suite door. "Hello? Devon, we're here."

Sam froze. *Fuck. Fuck. Fuck!* He did a quick scan. He could dive behind the couch and pray he didn't get spotted or…he moved to the door and opened it before the women could.

There were three Kitty Cats standing on the other side, looking a little stunned that it wasn't Devon answering the door. "Devon's in the shower."

"Oh, okay," one of the Cats said.

"Maybe we'll just slip in there with him," another one added.

"Good idea." Sam nodded behind him. "Could you let him know I need a charger for my phone? I was snooping around here for one but couldn't find anything."

"Sure thing, Samuel," the third girl said with a wink. "Tell Lexi we've got things under control."

Sam didn't know what that meant, but he took it for more than just showing Devon a good time. He nodded then let himself out, breathing a sigh of relief that he hadn't blown his cover by doing something stupid like trying to hide. Back in the day, it wouldn't have been odd for Sam to be going in and out of Devon's room without explicit permission. He had to hope that the same rules applied now.

It was time to buddy up with the staff and get a few beads on what they knew about their employer. Sam walked past his cabin door and hesitated before leaving the hall. He needed to get a few hours of sleep if he was going to be any good in this investigation, but Devon was a night owl and his staff would be working hard to set things right and clean up now before the party got revved up again. He didn't want to lose a chance to get some intel.

And yet…he glanced back at the door. Lexi was in there. Sam could slip into bed beside her and curl around her body, wake her up in a few hours by rubbing his cock along her pussy.

His dick throbbed at that idea.

Or he could get his fucking head out of the gutter and do his job. With a sigh, he pushed himself down the second hall to the steps that would take him back to the deck. There was a story here and he was determined to get it. Time with Lexi would have to wait…for now.

Chapter Six

Lexi slipped back into her cabin to find Sam still splayed out and dead to the world, asleep on their bed. She'd woken to find him like that, snoring softly and completely oblivious to her movement. He'd been kind to her in the early hours of the morning, giving her a release she'd needed without taking pity on her fragile state. She should never have delayed her pain medication dose for so long. She was usually very diligent about taking her pills, but for the first time in over a year, she felt like she had a purpose. She had a real job to do—protecting Sabine, finding out what Devon was up to... Yeah, that felt like the right thing to be doing.

She'd set the Kitty Cats up with instructions. Get close to Devon, and stay close to Devon. They knew what to do with that kind of direction. Before the day was through, Lexi was certain she'd have some information.

She'd spent the last hour chatting with the cleaning staff. She'd gone with a damsel-in-distress approach at first, which typically worked well with the older workers, both male and female. She knew she had a sweet, innocent-looking face and could play dumb as well as any other Kitty Cat when the need arose. She'd 'accidentally' spilled some orange juice on the expensive-looking carpet in the dining hall and hadn't wanted to upset her host. She'd even managed a few tears. All it had taken was an offer to get on her hands and knees to help and she was in.

Lexi and Rose had chatted for an hour or so about all the crazy things that had happened on the yacht so far in her employment, which, for Rose, was nearly two years. Mr. Caldone was very specific about what he wanted and how he wanted things done. He often had men on board who Rose found to be frightening—big men with guns who barked orders and threatened staff. They'd threatened Mr. Caldone on occasion as well, but her boss always seemed to brush it off like it was nothing. Rose knew better. She said they were bad men—bad, scary men.

Even though the meetings with these men had been closed-door, Rose knew that they wanted her boss to do something for them. They wanted him to use his celebrity connections to broker some kind of deal. She didn't know the details, but she did think that if it happened, her boss would get very rich...more rich than he already was.

So Devon had a scheme that somehow involved Sabine and also a group of dangerous men of some sort. From what Lexi knew of Devon, if there was money involved and he had a chance to make some, he'd be in, no matter the potential consequences.

Sam sighed and rolled over, exposing his long, muscular and fully tattooed back. It was a beautiful black-and-gray piece featuring ravens in flight over a forest, with a close-up of one black beauty sitting on a branch with a knife in its beak. Lexi didn't know what the symbolism was for Sam but she wanted to. She wanted to know what all his tattoos meant. In fact, she couldn't quite get enough of staring at him as it was, like he was already an addiction she was going to have a hell of a time breaking when the weekend was over.

Sam's ass was just barely poking from the sheets, and he had those irresistible dimples that she had to kiss.

She climbed onto the bed then quickly straddled Sam's legs. Before he could fully wake up, she was bent over and lightly kissing his ass dimples. He stirred then turned slightly to the side, almost toppling her over in the process.

"Am I about to get a wake-up, Kitty-style?"

Lexi laughed as she ran her hands under the sheets and squeezed his ass. What a fine one it was. Muscular, but with enough cushion that it wasn't totally rock hard. Unlike his cock, which was now tenting the sheet to the side.

"How are you feeling?" He rolled over completely, moving her with his hands on her waist so that she was positioned on top of him, straddling his dick.

"Great! Like I slept for longer than two hours." She ran her hands up his torso, admiring the chest tattoo that was all black and shades of gray as well. This one depicted a scene with the grim reaper harvesting souls. Morbid, sure, but beautiful, all the same. All the figures looked like Renaissance sculptures or paintings with some weeping, some moaning, everyone but the reaper in apparent anguish. It told a story. It made Lexi want to learn more about what made Sam tick. The tattoo continued down one arm, with gravestones and gnarly looking trees. The other arm had some color—blues, reds, purples—but had a similar theme, darkness, despair, maybe loneliness as well. It spoke to her in ways she didn't quite understand but felt deep down in her soul.

Sam held her waist. "You don't sleep much, do you?"

"No, not usually." She tapped her head. "Can't really get myself out of here. Bad dreams. Bad memories."

He nodded but didn't say anything more. He wasn't looking at her with pity either, though, so that was a good sign.

She rolled her hips, grinding her pussy against his cock. "I thought we could go for round two."

His eyes hooded. "So why are you still wearing clothes?"

His voice rumbled through her, all gravel and sand—so rough that she was surprised her clothes didn't just fall right off her body.

He leaned up, his abs engaging so his muscles were on display, and helped her pull off her top. She wasn't wearing a bra—didn't need one, really—and as soon as her breasts were exposed, Sam's eyes dilated and he got a hungry look on his face that made her shiver. He moved his hands down her body, using his thumbs to flick her throbbing nipples before resting his hands on her waist. He pulled her closer as he sat up so their upper bodies were touching, then he kissed her— devoured her, more like it. Sam was very skilled with his lips. His kiss was a lightning bolt that ignited every lusty nerve ending in her body. He caressed her mouth in a way that felt possessive, and she couldn't wait to find out what else he could do with his body.

His kiss was all consuming. He was inside her, sucking her, using his tongue to stroke her mouth and make her feel…what? Loved? *Hardly.* They barely knew each other. Not loved but desired, cherished, wanted in a way that her clients had never made her feel. She wasn't being paid to be here. This was a choice, and for the first time in a long time, she felt completely in control of what was happening to her body. Not that she didn't have a choice when she was with her clients, but this was different, special and something she craved more than anything.

He moved his hands down her back, brushing over her scar, making her freeze, but he didn't stop. He didn't linger on that ugly, bubbled flesh. He kept his hands sliding down to her ass then shifted her forward, so she rubbed against him right where he needed it.

She wanted no barriers between them. She needed to feel his flesh against hers. As if reading her mind, he tugged at the elastic of her leggings and somehow, without breaking their kiss, managed to help her get them off her hips and down her thighs. They had to move apart so she could strip them off her legs, and he did the honors of removing her panties.

He ran his fingers over her slit, rubbing her clit with the same slow stroke that he'd used when he'd been kissing her. She loved a long build and was in no rush to end things too quickly. She'd always found Sam hot and charismatic. He was dangerous territory, though, primarily because of his reporter status, but now he was even more dangerously intriguing because of his crime family connection.

The tattoos, the beard… It was all delicious, and that he didn't treat her like she was a broken thing thrilled her. He wrapped one arm around her waist and flung her onto her back. It wasn't rough, but it wasn't gentle either, and she liked it. He slipped his fingers into his mouth, licking away her juice. He closed his eyes, seemingly savoring her taste.

She reached down and took his cock into her hand, loving the heavy weight of it in her palm. He moaned and slipped his fingers out of his mouth then rubbed his saliva over her nipples, alternating between one sensitive nub and the other. He tweaked and flicked, ramping her up while she did the same to him, stroking and rubbing along his shaft.

He leaned down, trapping her hand between them, her fingers still wrapped tightly around his cock. He brushed his lips against her jaw, kissing his way to her ear. "I want to fuck your sweet pussy, Lexi," he growled. "I want to pound you hard and fast."

"Yes," she moaned. "Hard and fast."

"Condom?"

"Always."

"Good." He slipped off her and padded to the closet.

She admired the view. His fine ass, his rock-hard cock… They made her body tingle and her lusty excitement go into overdrive. She always traveled with condoms and had some in her bag as well. She had a feeling that before the weekend was over, they'd use every one they had.

He walked back with the condom on his cock then climbed onto the bed. He grabbed her hands, capturing them in one of his, and yanked them over her head so her body was pulled taut. He kissed her briefly, nudging her pussy with his cock. She opened her legs, spreading herself wide before wrapping her legs over his hips and urging him to do as he'd promised and pound her hard.

Sam cupped her ass and pushed her up as he entered her in one fluid glide. He was big, wide and stretched her out most deliciously. He gave her body a few seconds to adjust before pulling back almost to the tip then ramming her with such force that she cried out, her whole body shifting, almost making her head hit the headboard.

She tightened her grip with her legs, crossing her ankles over his back, and braced herself for the pussy drilling he'd promised. Every stroke rubbed her clit in just the right way. He rolled his hips then pulled her closer, grunting roughly each and each time he pounded into her. It was hard. It was brutal. It was exactly what she needed.

She was writhing before long, her nerve-endings sparking as her orgasm rose. She wanted to make it last forever — needed Sam to fuck her senseless.

Her back twitched, jolts of muscle pain that were so familiar to her battling with the pleasure of Sam fucking her. As if sensing her discomfort, Sam leaned down and bit her shoulder at the same time as he dug his fingers into her ass and pulled her even tighter to his body. She cried out again, the mix of pain and pleasure so intense in that moment that her climax peaked, and she moaned through her release. Her body zinged with cascading waves of pure bliss.

Sam grunted again, stroking her in a frenzy, his cock so rigid that it was like being pounded by a piece of steel. He bellowed his release, his dick thudding and twitching deep inside her.

He collapsed next to her, his body slick with sweat.

Her body hurt, but it was a good kind of hurt — the kind she'd been missing. The ache that had been hammering at her for months had lessened. Sam had fucked her so good that for the first time in a long time, she felt whole again, unbroken, normal.

"I am very, very satisfied." She turned onto her side so she could drape an arm over his stomach and rest her head on his chest. It was intimate, sure, but she wanted to at least pretend that there was more between them.

"I am too." He ran his hand along her arm then down to her back.

She flinched. A nervous tic.

"Does it hurt to touch?" He hovered over her scar, his fingers skimming around but not *on* the reminder of her wounds.

"No. Not really." She traced her fingers over his abs, watching him tighten up as she glided over his muscles. "Sometimes if the water is too hot in the shower, it's sensitive."

He let his hand drop, covering part of her scar with his palm. "This why you retired?"

She cleared her throat. Inevitably, most people wanted to know how she'd injured herself. The gag order-confidentiality agreement prevented her from saying much publicly about that hellish day — or the hellish ones that had followed — but that wasn't why she didn't like talking about what had happened. There was so much emotion tied up in that memory that it drained her to go through the details.

"It's part of the reason." She sighed. "I was doing a new routine and I — "

"You don't have to tell me." He lifted his hand and brushed some hair from her face. "That's not why I was asking."

She was stunned into silence. That was not the reaction she had been expecting.

"I was only wondering about the pain and how you're managing it—how far you want to go with this between us. I can get rough—as rough as you need me to be."

Lexi shifted herself so she could look at him. "The pain-pleasure dynamic is strange, isn't it?" She felt like he knew about this somehow. If she were going to guess, she would put money on his tattoos being an outlet for him. He understood pain the way she did. Complicated didn't even begin to describe what she needed. Her pain could be debilitating at times, and yet the right kind of pain, the sexual kind, could be so freeing that it took all the other pain away. Not many people could wrap their heads around that.

"It is." He rubbed his thumb over her bottom lip. "I want you to feel good. Satisfied."

She wished she could keep this guy. He was all kinds of amazing. "I can handle a lot." Pain was her therapy. It helped her sorrow come to the surface and evaporate.

He nodded once. "Okay then. Safeword?"

She smiled. "Lucky."

"Yeah, feels that way." He pulled her up his body and kissed her hard.

This weekend will be one I won't be forgetting any time soon.

Chapter Seven

Sam left their room only to make sure that Devon was still asleep and so that he could collect a few supplies he'd need to make this weekend unforgettable for Lexi. She wanted pain, so he'd give it to her in all the sexy ways he could.

Lexi was in the shower. Next time he'd join her, but right now he wanted to set the room up as a dungeon of pleasure for her enjoyment. He lowered the blackout blinds that he'd learned from the housekeeper were available at a click of a button and lit the candles he'd found. He set out his tools — items easily found around a house, or in this case, a yacht, to be used for sexual play. Even though it was almost midday, the cabin was dark with the eerie glow of flickering candles, which made it seem dangerous and sensual at the same time.

He'd ordered lunch to be delivered while Lexi was in the shower, and the food had arrived, adding the aroma of garlic and rosemary, among other things.

Devon spared no expense with his guests, and Sam had taken full advantage.

"Oh, it smells delicious in here." She walked out of the steaming bathroom completely naked, her hair still wet and plastered to her body.

She was something else, truly, and he wanted to throw her onto the bed and fuck her brains out, but he restrained himself, even though his pants were tenting uncomfortably, so he held up the neckties he'd found.

A slow smile spread on her face and she held her wrists toward him without question. But he had other plans. He motioned for her to follow him into the walk-in closet, where hooks lined the walls. He tied each of her wrists so that she was secured to them, her arms outstretched but bent slightly. Then he pulled a handkerchief out of his back pocket and covered her eyes, tying it tightly behind her head.

"Are you hungry, Lexi?" He brushed his body against hers, knowing his clothing would rub her skin in all the right ways.

"Starving." She nodded then bit her bottom lip.

"Good." He left the closet and collected his first set of treats, bringing a tray and stand to the door of the closet. "I hope you like sushi."

"Love it."

He used the chopsticks to pick up a piece of the California roll and offered it to her.

"Mmmm."

As she was chewing, he wrapped an elastic band around the chopsticks, rigging them to act as a clamp. He rubbed his fingers gently over her budded nipple and she moaned around the sushi roll.

"Time for a little pain, Lexi." He positioned the chopsticks and quickly secured them with another elastic.

Lexi bucked, hissing out a moan when the chopsticks bit down on her nipple.

Sam grabbed the second pair, picked up another piece of sushi and offered it to her. "Still hungry?"

"Mmm-hmm." She nodded, even though her face had turned a nice shade of pink and her chest was heaving from her heavy breaths.

He offered her the sushi then quickly clamped her other nipple. She groaned through her mouthful of food, her body undulating as she swayed a bit in her restraints.

He turned back to his tray and fished out an ice cube from the water. He let it drip over her chest, watching as the droplets rolled down her sternum to her belly. She gasped then yelped when he placed the ice cube directly onto her nipple.

"Something to soothe your aching nips." He moved the ice from one clamp to the other, knowing that he was preventing Lexi's body from growing accustomed to the clamps. Her nipples may have started to numb from the pressure that was on them, but right now, with the ice directly on her flesh, she would be feeling the pinch like he'd just put the clamps there.

She was biting her bottom lip again, something he found so fucking sexy.

"Ohhh, you're dripping water everywhere." He leaned down and flicked his tongue over her ice-cold nipple, knowing that the heat of his breath, of his touch, would send jolts through her entire body. She writhed beneath him, trying to pull away, which made him all the more determined to tease her.

He moved his tongue to the other nipple so he could put the ice on the one he'd just left. Then he alternated again and again and again, until Lexi was moaning loudly, bucking her hips as if she were going to come already.

He pulled himself back and dropped the ice cube on the tray, then he guided her so she could flip over. The ties had enough give to cross, but they pulled her body taut, so she was forced to arch her back in order to keep her head up.

It was the perfect position for what he wanted to do next. She was ass up and on full display. And what an ass it was, heart-shaped and flawless. He leaned down then nipped at her skin. Another day he might leave bite marks, but for now, pulling another yelp of surprise out of her was satisfying enough.

He picked up the wooden spoon next.

She moved toward him, angling herself as though she expected another bite. Instead, he brought the spoon down with a slap. She groaned. Her ass cheek went instantly red, and her body swayed forward with the force. But she pushed back again for more. He reached around to cup her pussy, digging his fingers into her slit, then he smacked her again. The sound of the spoon hitting her flesh made his cock weep. She was so responsive, her pussy was soaked and she rolled her hips when he put pressure on her clit with the heel of his palm. *Fuck*, she was so hot and ready for him.

He whacked her a few more times on that side of her ass then switched to the other cheek. Instead of cupping her pussy, he went right for her clit, fingering the nub roughly as he swatted her. Her skin was so pale that each wallop left its mark, red imprints that excited Sam as much as feeling her clit did, all hard and swollen, throbbing under his fingers.

He dropped the spoon back on the tray then used both hands to squeeze her cheeks, rubbing the sting in, kneading her flesh that was so sensitive until she was moaning nonstop, her hips moving, begging him with her body for a good fucking.

Who am I to deny that?

"You want my big fat cock in your pussy?" He was already unzipping his pants, too impatient to strip. He let his pants drop to the floor and swiped a condom from the tray. He had a pile there, knowing he'd be fucking her repeatedly until they were both spent.

She hadn't stopped moaning, but now she was nodding too, trying to look at him over her shoulder, even though she was still blindfolded.

He sheathed himself with the latex then with Lexi. He pounded into her fast and firm, taking her completely, not giving her time to adjust, just pulling out again and ramming right back in. It was literal seconds before they were both coming—spasming, loudly moaning, explosively fast orgasms that left them panting, their bodies flushed and coated in a sheen of sweat. Sam was nowhere close to being done, though.

He pulled out, then yanked the condom off before dropping it to the garbage. He rolled Lexi over so that the ties weren't crossed and her arms had some range again. She was still panting, her beautiful breasts heaving. She'd say the safeword if she was at her limit, but Sam guessed that she was nowhere close.

Her nipples were so red that they looked like they were giving off heat. He lightly brushed the chopsticks, tugging them a little in order to get a reaction. Lexi hissed but didn't pull away, so he did it again, tugging a bit harder on the sticks, pulling her nipples a tad more. The pain etched on her beautiful face was a total turn-on. His cock was hard and desperately wanting to sink back into her soaking pussy.

But Sam had other plans.

He picked up the candle, which had pooled a good amount of wax already, then angled her body, one hand under her, holding her back up so she had support and so that the wax wouldn't travel far. He watched her face closely as he tipped the candle, letting a few drops of wax fall to her stomach.

She moaned, then sighed. He dripped more wax over her torso. She bit her bottom lip again, a sign to keep going. He moved the candle higher and let a stream of wax fall onto the tops of her breasts. Her nipples were primed, ready to be sucked…but not yet.

Sam moved the candle to Lexi's side and let the wax dribble along her waist. She writhed, pulled herself this way and that, trying to get away—but not really. He put the candle down before running his hands over her body, releasing the dried wax from her skin to reveal red marks. He scooped out an ice cube and retraced his movements, circling the cold over her wax burns. Goosebumps rose in the path of the ice, and water dripped down her body. Sam wanted to lick her from head to toe.

He moved the ice up to her nipples, circling there, making her moan. He ran a fingernail over her captured buds, and she hissed loudly, so he stuck the ice cube in her mouth then got to work unlatching the clamps.

He released one nipple and immediately sucked it into his mouth, rolling the hot little nub around, coating it in his saliva and flicking away the burn of release. All the same, Lexi shuddered, letting out quiet whimpers around the ice in her mouth. Sam watched her squirm as he ran the pad of his thumb over the other nipple, the one that was still clamped. She looked completely anguished, totally tortured and unbelievably sexy. He gave one last tugging suck on her nipple in his mouth then let go. He wanted to be inside her when he let the other nipple loose.

He donned another condom, then flipped Lexi over again so her ass was in the air. He didn't give her time to think too long because he slipped inside, hard and fast. He ran his hands up her body, slipping under so he could unlatch the remaining clamp. He was slow, methodical, rolling his body and stroking her pussy as he removed the elastic from one side of the chopsticks. She was making a sexy-as-fuck mewing sound that made him want to pound her harder, but he knew she needed a slow burn, like what her nipples probably felt when he released them from the clamps and all the blood rushed back to them.

As soon as her nipple was free, she bucked into him, arching her back and tilting her head so that he could grab her hair, fisting it in one hand. He rubbed at her nipple with the other hand, rolling the bud between his fingers and thumb

She pushed back harder, clearly wanting him to go deeper. He curled her hair around his fist tightly then pulled his cock partly out. "You ready for this, baby?"

She moaned a yes.

He rammed her good and hard, pumping her as fast as he could while still playing with her tit and keeping a strong grip on her hair.

He knew he was hurting her, but with that pain came pleasure, and by the sounds she was making, Lexi was enjoying every bit of his attention.

"Yes, Sam! Yesyesyesyesyes!"

He tried to hold off, to keep his orgasm from cresting, but it was just too fucking hot and her pussy was so crazy wet and tight. She spasmed, her body quivering, letting him know that she was close too. He let go of her hair, watching as it cascaded over her shoulders to hang around her face like a veil. Slipping his hand down her front, he put his fingers to work on her clit. Seconds later, she was screaming through another orgasm, her whole body shaking. His cock exploded right along with her, spewing cum into the condom so hard that he was sure the thing would bust open.

He rode her until every last shudder had stopped, and yet her pussy kept clenching him hard, like she didn't want him to pull out. *Fuck*, he could stay there forever.

Best fuck of the century.

She was panting and laughing, and so was he.

"Whoa!" She turned a bit as if to look over her shoulder at him.

He reached forward, his cock still embedded inside her, and undid the blindfold. "Good?"

She nodded slowly. "Very." Her eyes were dazed and her smile lazy, like her brain had truly been fucked out of her head.

He pulled his cock out before discarding the condom. "Let's go eat the rest of this stuff in bed."

"Mmmm, yes please." She ran her hands down her torso, stopping just above her pussy. "Everything is tingling." She looked down at herself then smiled when she looked back up at him. "You did a number on me."

Lexi's body showed the marks of Sam's attention. There were red splotches where the wax had burned, and her nipples were still bright pink and budded prettily. He trailed his eyes over her ass as she moved out of the closet before climbing onto the bed. There were nice-looking welts from the spoon marking her skin there too.

"That wasn't too much?" He knew the answer but felt compelled to ask anyway. It was hard not to see Lexi as vulnerable with all the delicate features she had, and added to that, the bubbling scar tissue that spoke of major trauma. He picked up the tray of food then carried it to the bed.

"It was perfect."

He propped up a couple of pillows for her, then adjusted some for himself before climbing up into the bed next to her, the tray of food laid out for them. "I wasn't sure if you liked oysters, but they were available, so I figured why not?"

"Not my favorite, no." She picked up an olive and popped it into her mouth. "But the sushi is amazing." She bypassed the package of chopsticks and picked up the sushi with her fingers. "It helps me," she said, waving the sushi around. "To welcome the pain like that. To invite it. You know?" She popped the roll into her mouth.

"Yeah, I do know." He ran his hand over his chest, rubbing where he remembered the most pain, both inside and out. "Getting inked helps me with that too."

She nodded, her mouth full of sushi.

"I probably sound like a poor little rich kid saying this, but growing up with the kind of money my folks have… It creates expectations and pressure."

"I can imagine." She grabbed a handful of cashews. "More so probably because of the crime element."

Exactly. He closed his eyes. "I didn't realize how bad it was — how bad they were and still are. I grew up in a bubble, thinking that it was normal for a family to be guarded by a dozen men with guns at all hours of the day and night. I thought nothing of having personal security with me wherever I went. Then the show happened, and I realized how fucked up it all was. My family played up the crime boss stuff too, made it mainstream in some ways. It was all bullshit, though. My family is one-hundred-percent into white-collar crime, extortion to some degree, intimidation and threats, but as far as I know, they aren't murderers. They never came out and said on the show that we did that kind of thing, but all the same, people were writing emails and sending mail that idolized my family for things that should have brought the FBI knocking on our door. I guess because nothing was ever admitted outright." Sam sighed.

It was all so complicated. He'd left his family because of that shit. It had been too much to handle and so far from normal that Sam hadn't been able to take it any longer. His father had expected him to pick up the reins and take over the operations, but Sam had had other plans. "There was one episode… I'd come home from college for the weekend and they were filming — "

"You were on the show?" She nearly choked on a fig.

He snorted, reaching over to pat her back. "It's not worth choking over. Trust me."

She took a sip of water. "I wouldn't have guessed you'd be on that show."

"I'll take that as a compliment." He brushed his fingers through his hair and tugged at the elastic, pulling it free so the waves cascaded to his shoulders. "There are a few episodes that I'm in, actually. It was in the contract that I'd make appearances every eight episodes or something. They cut scenes to make me look a certain way."

"Like how?" She leaned closer, her eyes intensely focused on him.

"Oh, you know, the calm, highly intellectual, reasonable one." He snorted again. "I think the audience felt I was a giant pussy, though. I never got into it with my folks or my cousins on camera, and anytime they started to get me riled up, I walked away. The director made it work so that I was the strong, silent one, apparently exceptionally deadly. They caught me one day out with Dad at the shooting range. I'm a pretty good shot — and that turned into a storyline for them, like I was some kind of hitman for my family or something."

"Maybe I should watch the show." She winked.

"Please don't." He laughed. "I was very much a pretty boy back then — clean cut, fully shaved, golf shirts."

Her eyes went wide. "Now I really want to see an episode."

He pulled her into his arms and kissed her all the while she giggled like a maniac. "It's not a good look for me."

She stopped laughing and put her hand on the side of his face. "I like your look." She moved closer, her eyes still locked on his. "Thank you for taking care of me today."

"It was my pleasure." His voice came out all gravelly.

"And mine." She kissed him—just a soft, gentle kiss, but it made his heart thunder and his head swim. "I hope you'll do it again before the weekend is over."

"That is something I can definitely promise." He wrapped his arm around her and pulled her close. "I'd like to maybe keep you—"

Someone knocked hard on the door.

Sam got up quickly and threw on a pair of boxers. Lexi was already covering up with a sheet.

"Yo, Samuel. Open up!" Devon's booming voice vibrated through the door.

Sam opened it enough to shield Lexi as much as possible. "What's up, man?"

"Here." He thrust a charger at him, his gaze roving in search of Lexi, no doubt. "The girls said you were looking for one."

"Right. I was." He took the charger. "Thanks."

"You two still sleeping? Fuck, get your asses out of bed. We've got an excursion planned for tonight!"

"What excursion?" Sam was wary. He knew the ship had been moving all night but hadn't checked to see where they were headed.

"Key West, baby!" Devon pulled his sunglasses over his bloodshot eyes. "I rented a place there so we can par-tay." He lowered his voice. "Actually, I meant to tell you last night. Hey, could you come out here a minute?"

Sam looked over his shoulder at Lexi and said, "Be right back," before stepping out with Devon. "What did you mean to tell me?"

"I've set up a meeting for you" — he pulled off his sunglasses and started fidgeting with them — "with a couple of my associates who want to talk to you."

Sam's hackles rose. "What associates?" he growled.

Devon raised his hands. "Whoa, man. There's no need to get all pissed. I've been hanging with these dudes who are, like, in love with your dad or something. They want an intro."

"An intro." Sam crossed his arms. "Like I'm some kind of fucking celebrity who wants fans?"

Devon still had his hands up. "I know. I know. I had to —" He leaned in closer. "These dudes, they do some good work. I think you'll want to hear what they have to say."

"Who are they?"

Devon grinned. "Not who you think. Trust me. You're going to like these guys."

"Devon…"

He was already walking down the hall, his sunglasses back on. "Limo leaves in an hour. Be ready. Oh, and tell your girl that she's sitting next to me at dinner. It's my turn to get to know her."

Key West. Fuck. Sam went back into the stateroom and closed the door but didn't turn around. There were so many bad possibilities when it came to the *dudes* Devon wanted Sam to meet. If he weren't a reporter, hungry for a story, he'd blow this meeting off completely, but now he was pissed *and* intrigued, and that was a shitty combination for his mental health and general wellbeing. He ran his hand through his hair as he turned around, tugging at the knots in frustration.

"Is everything okay, Sam?" The bed creaked as Lexi moved toward him.

"Devon's got something cooked up that involves my dad somehow. He wants me to meet with gang leaders or crime bosses or something. He was being irritatingly vague."

Lexi's eyes widened. "That sounds ominous."

"Yeah, no shit, right?" He flashed a grin at her. "You bring a sexy dress with you?"

Chapter Eight

"I need a sexy dress for your meeting?" Lexi wasn't stupid. There was a glint in Sam's eyes when he was excited about something. Right now he might be angry at Devon, but he was also intrigued by whatever Devon had told him — and Lexi was coming along for the ride.

"Right, yes, this might be dangerous. Shit!" Sam paced away from the door and Lexi let the sheets that were covering her fall away so she could get up too.

"Hey, you wanna fill me in on what's going on?" She used her soft voice, the one she knew would calm any beast of a man. "Maybe I can help."

"Devon's set up a meeting between me and some dudes." He air-quoted the last word. "They're after a connection to my father, so you know we're not talking about upstanding citizens."

"You expected that, though." Lexi perched herself on the corner of the bed.

"I overheard him talking on the phone last night when I went to his room." Sam held up the charger.

"He came in while I was searching, and I managed to hide in the bathroom before he saw me."

"Very stealth." She winked.

He cracked a smile, the flash of anger she'd seen seconds ago slipping away. "Well, it was stealth until your Kitty Cats came to the door. I figured, better to make up some excuse than get caught trying to hide in the curtains or whatever." He laughed. "So I opened the door and invited them in."

"Smooth." Lexi nodded toward the charger. "I'm guessing he's none-the-wiser."

Now Sam really laughed. "You've met Devon, right?"

Lexi laughed along with him. "Right."

"He's after Sabine." Sam's smile fell away again. "And he's going to try to get to her through you."

"I figured." She tapped her head. "I'm not as stupid as people think I am. None of the Cats are."

"I never thought you were stupid."

He sounded offended, like she'd hurt his feelings for even suggesting that he thought that way about her.

"Many men do, though, so it's usually a safe assumption." She shrugged. "He asked for me specifically. He wants me here. You've cockblocked him a couple of times already. I'm sure he's anxious to pick my fluffy brain." She giggled in an exaggerated way, then rolled her eyes. "I'm in the inner circle, aren't I? Close to Sabine."

He cracked a smile, but it was fleeting. Then he started pacing. "It's dangerous. We're entering territory that could lead to trouble." He winced. "I put out a few requests to confidential sources last night, people who may have some idea what's going on with Devon, but I haven't heard back yet. I talked to the staff a bit, but they didn't have much to say to me. I need to get Devon alone. Have some guy time."

"I've got the Cats on him." Lexi moved to the closet and got a shiver at the memory of what he'd done to her in there. Her body was still sore in all the right ways, tiny reminders every time she moved that would be with her all night. "They'll check in as soon as they can safely do so." She slipped on a pair of panties, then thought better on it and pulled them back off. Her black dress was form-fitting and she liked to go bare when wearing it. She grabbed it from the hanger and unzipped the back. She shimmied into it, running her hands down her sides to smooth out the fabric. It fit her like a glove, hugging every part of her body. She walked out of the closet with a pair of heels dangling from her hand.

Sam was standing there contemplating her, his hand stroking that fine beard of his. "So what's your strategy?"

She turned her back to him. "Zip me up, please."

He ran his finger gently down her spine, which gave her another shiver. Her whole body tingled whenever he laid his hands on her. "Your Cats will be discreet?"

She glanced over her shoulder, her expression answering such an asinine question.

"Right." He chuckled then zipped her up. "These guys we're meeting... If they're who I suspect, it's a shaky alliance between two shitheads who move drugs through the Keys, up the coast and into the noses of every partier in South Florida and probably beyond, at this point.

"Rose said they're bad news. That they carry guns at all times and threaten Devon regularly." Lexi bent down to put her shoes on, wincing a little at the stiffness of her back.

"Who's Rose?" Sam knelt in front of her and took the shoe out of her hand. Without missing a beat, he gently slipped one on, then the other. She braced herself with his shoulders.

"Thank you." She should be embarrassed. That would be her usual reaction to someone helping her like that, but strangely, she wasn't. Sam knew what she needed, like he was reading her at every moment. "Rose is one of the cleaners. I chatted with her while you were sleeping. I think she knows more but she was too scared to really get into it with me. She said that Devon had a meeting recently with 'the bad men' and they were doing a lot of yelling about getting things done or else. It scared her enough to ask for a sick day, the first one she's ever taken in eighteen years of working as a cleaner for various yacht owners."

"Guns are not out of the ordinary in Florida, but if these are the drug runners I'm thinking of, then yeah, we've got something to be worried about." He finished slipping on her second shoe, then ran his hands over her hips as he straightened. "I'll make sure I'm sitting on the other side of you at that dinner table."

"No, we need to split up. Let me work on Devon." She batted her eyelashes, earning a cocked eyebrow from Sam. "This is what I've been trained to do. I'm good at getting information out of powerful men. Trust me." Or, at least, she *used* to be good at it. "His guard will be down with me."

Sam looked skeptical. Not surprising really, considering that the inner workings of the Kitty Cats were kept very secret. She'd have her doubts too if she were an outsider looking in. But what came out of his mouth was refreshingly different from her assumptions. "Considering I couldn't get a lot out of the staff myself, I'd say you're probably better to do the covert interviewing. Just know that I've got your back."

She leaned up so she could kiss him, which he deepened with his skillful tongue. "You should know that I'm not wearing panties," she whispered once their kiss ended.

Sam reached around to grab her ass with both hands, squeezing her enough for her to feel the welts he'd left from the spoon. "And that's why we make a good team."

She laughed. *Are we a team?* Sam had always been off limits as far as the Kitty Cats were concerned. Sabine had been pretty explicit in warning them against ever talking to him about any details related to the organization. And yet, she knew that Sabine thought very highly of him. She'd feed him stories that she wanted expert coverage on, even if the information was damaging to her personally. Bad press was good publicity. Even though Lexi wasn't technically a Kitty Cat anymore, she was definitely going to hold back any information that might hurt her ex-boss' reputation. So, Sam might think they were partners in this, but Lexi had to keep him out of the loop if the need arose, at least until she could touch base with Sabine or even Adam, her head of security, for direction before she took any action.

And that made her feel very torn. She liked Sam…a lot—not only because he did fantastic things to her body but also because he was in control, intelligent and seemed to get her on so many different levels. She wanted to be partners with him.

"Okay, I guess I better put some more clothes on." He let her go with a smack on her ass then turned to survey the room. "What do you need before we go? Your purse?"

"I carry some meds in there, just in case." She beelined for the small clutch she liked to use.

"But you don't like using them." His voice was muffled, and she realized he'd gone into the closet. When he remerged a few minutes later, he was wearing black dress pants and a blue button-up shirt. Classy yet casual. He looked gorgeous.

"I have to use them and that pisses me off. I have to take them every damn night at least. But as long as I don't do anything stupid, I can usually get away with only taking a few." She actually had to take double doses some nights, even when she didn't do anything stupid, like twisting her back, lifting something that was not even the least bit heavy, bending over…or ofttimes just existing.

"So gymnastics of any kind is out." He moved to the bathroom and quickly tied his hair, half up, half down. She loved his hair like that. It made him look like a total badass.

"Yes." She gulped back the lump that always seemed to appear when her mind shifted to what she used to be able to do. "I can't move that way anymore."

When he walked out of the bathroom, he came straight for her, encircling her waist and pulled her up against his body with a tight hold. "I like your moves." He kissed her again, and boy, she could so get used to this. "Maybe you're destined to be an investigative reporter."

She laughed. "I don't have the patience for writing."

"Well, then maybe you're destined to be my sidekick."

She gave a fake gasp of shock then swatted his arm. "Sidekick?"

He laughed as he nuzzled her neck, making her melt all over again. "Okay, okay, you can be the lead."

"No, I like it better when you lead," she said just before he trailed his lips to her mouth and kissed her.

He made her feel so warm and fuzzy, which banished the self-pity she was used to feeling when her thoughts turned to what she'd lost. Those warm fuzzies were dangerous territory. She didn't want to make the mistake of falling for a guy like Sam. He wasn't a keeper, even if she wanted him to be. She wasn't cut out for long-term relationships — not now, maybe not ever. She was too broken for that.

He lingered on her lips, giving her a thorough kissing before letting her go. "Ready for this?"

She nodded.

"Anything gets weird, like pushes your limits, and we leave. Okay?"

"Agreed."

"Whatever we find out tonight, it determines what we do next." Sam entwined his fingers with hers. "I want a story out of this, and I know there's a juicy one just waiting to be uncovered."

Lexi nodded and pasted on a smile, even though her insides were all twisted up with guilt. If it came down to it, Lexi would protect her boss, *ex-boss*, even from Sam. There was no way she'd let him have a story that might damage Sabine or put her life at risk.

And that was why she would never get to keep him.

* * * *

The mansion that Devon had rented was the biggest one on the beach. It was all glass and jutting angles of white steel, making it look like a piece of art as much as a beach house. When they'd pulled up in the limo, they could already hear the music pounding and they hadn't even stepped out of the car yet. Sam had exchanged a look with her. *Maybe there won't be a lot of opportunity for conversation after all*, was what his expression had said. She'd just winked. The Kitty Cats were on it.

"Did you get anything?" Lexi asked Tanya as she dabbed on a little more lip gloss.

Lexi and the other Kitty Cats had made for one of the main floor washrooms as soon as they'd arrived. It was standard practice when they were tag-teaming a client. Like most mansions, the washrooms were massive and could accommodate four women who needed to share intel and makeup.

"We all got a little bit of something." Tanya passed Noel, one of the other Cats, a compact. "But after I passed out, it was Noel who really got the dirt."

Noel grinned. "That guy won't shut up. He brags about everything from his huge cock to his huge bank account."

"And his cock is nothing I haven't seen before," Courtney laughed. "Hardly worth bragging about, if you ask me." She wet a towel and dabbed the back of her neck. "This heat is unreal. I'm sweating just standing around."

Even with the air conditioning blasting, Lexi knew what Courtney meant. She'd come to accept the constant sheen of sweat on her skin, though.

"There will be men coming tonight. Important men," Noel continued. "Sounds like gang affiliation, but not any gang I've ever heard before. The Riders and the Highwaymen?"

"Bikers, maybe?" Courtney shrugged.

"Devon made it sound like they were pirates. No joke," Noel said. "Or like a gang of Robin Hoods or something."

"Why would a wealthy socialite like Devon Caldone want to associate with two gangs like that?" Lexi couldn't make the pieces fit with what Sam had said earlier. Pirate drug runners who stole from the rich and gave to the poor? *Huh?*

"Makes sense if they're after Sabine, which they are," Tanya added. She cocked her hip out and leaned on the vanity. "He has a hate-on for her something awful. Says she's too arrogant for her own good and thinks she's above the law…which to him means the gang law or something, because he clearly doesn't have a problem associating with criminals. I definitely got the impression that this isn't only about her blowing him off at a couple of parties."

"No, it's definitely more than that." Lexi handed the lip gloss back to Tanya. "You upload this information to the system yet?" Sabine had a database where she collected all the big and small tidbits the Cats had collected over the years. The secrets she had could make or break careers and could certainly destroy empires.

"Yep. It was the first thing we did when Devon went to go chew out some staff." Tanya clicked her purse closed.

Lexi knew she should tell the girls about Sam's real identity, but she hesitated. She maybe wasn't a Cat, but that didn't mean her loyalties had changed. The thing holding her back was the promise she'd made to keep the real life of Samuel Dove a secret, even from Sabine. Under any other circumstance, while she was a Cat, a promise like that to a man wouldn't have stopped her from sharing what she knew with Sabine, but now? Well, she just wasn't sure she could betray Sam. No, she *was* sure. She wouldn't betray him. She couldn't do that to him.

Which is why it's a bad idea to get involved with a guy like Sam, stupid.

"Devon thinks he'll get something out of me tonight about Sabine. Not sure what, but I'm guessing I'll have stuff for you to upload once the night is over." Lexi hadn't checked, but she was fairly certain that her access to the database had ended the moment she'd handed in her retirement papers. "I'll compile it in a folder and send it to you as soon as I can."

Tanya made a face like she was confused but quickly seemed to figure it out. "You think Sabine kicked you out of the database?" Tanya shook her head. "I doubt that very much. She'll never stop thinking of you as a Cat, Lexi. I bet you can log in right now."

Lexi wanted to argue, but a small part of her wanted Tanya to be right.

"There's an airport limo coming to get us in an hour. We'll be able to stick around and keep our ears open until then."

"Sounds good. Be safe."

"Of course," Tanya said then blew Lexi a kiss. "We'll see you in New York at some point."

Lexi nodded as she watched the other women file out. She'd miss this—the sisterhood, the espionage, the intrigue. She might as well enjoy it while she could.

She lifted her phone and clicked onto the app that Adam had created for the Kitty Cats to collect data. She let her finger hover over the icon. She wanted to click it but she didn't, at the same time. If Sabine had kicked her out of the program, she wouldn't get past the first screen. Did she really wanted to know?

Lexi swallowed her trepidation and clicked the icon. The app loaded, prompting for her password. With a deep sigh, she quickly typed in the eight-alpha code.

And the database loaded.

Lexi smiled, a warm feeling of belonging rolling over her. Sabine hadn't kicked her out yet. She was still a Cat for now.

"Time to get in the game, Lexi-girl." She checked her reflection one last time. "You've got this."

Chapter Nine

"Samuel Dove," the burly, bearded leader of the Riders, Vince Cutter, said, his hand out to shake. "I've heard a lot about you. Of course, I know your family by reputation."

Sam shook Vince's hand. The biker was dressed in a casual suit, cut to his substantial frame and screaming of money, but there was an underlying roughness there, as one would expect from a known second-tier crime boss. There was no doubt in Sam's mind that Vince and all his crew in attendance were carrying, probably armed to the teeth. Thanks to Sam's upbringing and exposure to the criminal elements of the United States, he knew who Vince was on sight. He also knew that the Riders were best known for drug running and not much more. So why the fuck would Devon want Sam to meet with a guy like Vince? The Riders were nothing to Sam's father, at least not a gang that his father would want to work a deal with.

"Always good to meet friends of Devon." Sam nodded toward the tall, lanky dude who looked like a methhead ready for a fight and who was fast approaching the two of them. "He one of yours?"

Vince glanced to his left then flashed a scowl that was there and gone in an instant. "No. Not mine."

Devon swooped in as the lanky guy reached them. "Samuel, this is the other man I wanted to introduce you to. Dax Fury."

Ahhh, someone Sam had heard of but had never met. He was elusive, never photographed and newly leading the Highwaymen, an infamous Robin Hood-type gang. They'd started in e-commerce. They were criminal geeks who managed to rip off a ton of wealthy but shady investors without any repercussions then gave that money to various low-income social programs.

"Good to meet you."

Sam's reporter senses were binging. Dax Fury was the guy to meet. He'd been well known as a lieutenant for the Highwaymen for the last ten years until something had gone down the previous year that had dismantled the organization's leadership and had flipped it on its head. Dax had stepped in as leader and everyone had either fallen in line—or had disappeared. At least, that was what Sam had heard. He'd love to do an exclusive on Dax, but that would mean revealing his alter-ego. It wasn't like he could put on a pair of glasses to disguise himself either. That only worked in the comic books, unfortunately. But he wasn't out of the game yet. Something was going on there for the Highwaymen to ally with a low-life like Vince Cutter. When Devon had said he'd set up a meeting, Sam hadn't been thinking it would be with a guy like Dax, and he couldn't help but feel almost giddy at the prospect of infiltrating the Highwaymen in some way that he could exploit for an article. *Fuck, maybe a series of articles.*

The Highwaymen were notoriously difficult to work with, as one would expect, and had a very rigid code of conduct that resembled some kind of weird Robin Hood-type infrastructure. They not only donated to charities in an effort to appear law-abiding but actively looked for opportunities to exploit wealthy individuals, even going as far as to allegedly steal millions of dollars in cash and product, guns, drugs and women in order to fund their various fucked-up philanthropic pursuits.

The cherry on top of this particular cake was that the Highwaymen had been the bane of Sam's father's existence for the last twenty years. Not enough for the Dove family to do anything permanent—territory was territory and the Highwaymen were a force to be reckoned with—but enough for his father to swear profusely anytime the Highwaymen came up in conversation. Their ability to infiltrate and manipulate the dark web had all the old guard from Sam's father's generation extremely on edge. The fact that the Highwaymen could dismantle the wealth of anyone with a few clicks of their collective mice was enough to have every crime boss in the world tiptoeing around them. So far, though, they'd upheld some fucked-up moral code and hadn't touched any other crime syndicate.

"Dax," Vince said gruffly, the tone suggesting this was not an easy alliance or a steady one.

Dax all but ignored Vince, not even bothering to acknowledge him beyond a slight nod. "Samuel, I hope

Devon has filled you in on our ask. We're looking for a formal introduction to—"

"Dude! Have you taken a look around?" Devon draped his arm around Dax's shoulders...obviously missing the death glare he was getting from not only Dax but also from all the men he'd come with, who were milling about. "Women, booze, food. Let's enjoy ourselves before we talk business."

Sam didn't need Dax to finish his statement. He wanted a meeting with Sam's father or at least some kind of introduction, a bridge to his father's enterprise. *But why?*

"I've got a proposition for your dad," Dax continued as he shook off Devon's arm and gave him another warning glare.

"*We've* got a proposition," Vince interjected, sliding his own glare toward Dax.

"Well, fellas, I'd be happy to hear—"

"Hi, boys," Lexi's sexy purr interrupted all conversation as she slipped in next to Sam and wrapped her arm around his waist. She held her hand out to Dax. "I'm Lexi Monroe."

Dax gave her a scorching once-over before taking her hand and shaking it. Sam wanted to take exception, but he didn't own Lexi, no matter how much he wanted her to be only his. "You work for Sabine Cowan?"

Lexi smiled one of her bright, disarming smiles. "Used to. Now I work for myself."

Dax grunted as if he approved before glancing over at Devon. Sam was starting to piece all the players together. Sabine was the Highwaymen's next target. Her wealth was likely very enticing to the dark-web gang, but what did his father have to do with it all?

"Well, now that we all know each other, how about we get to the food part of the night? Lexi?" Devon pushed past Sam to claim Lexi, which once again had Sam's hackles rising.

He tamped it down. *Not yours to keep, stupid.*

"You're sitting next to me at the table tonight. I want to get to know the girl who stole my good pal Samuel's heart."

Lexi threw a look over her shoulder at Sam, letting him know that she had things under control. "Have I done that?" She giggled. "I thought I just stole his cock."

Devon laughed loudly as they walked off.

Dax closed in on Sam. "We have things to talk about."

Sam nodded, then motioned to the door. "Lead the way."

Lexi thought a formal dinner was such a strange thing for Devon to insist on, considering that he was hosting at least a hundred people at the Key West mansion. She soon figured out that only Devon's hand-picked guests had actual seats at the table. The rest of the guests were milling around, taking up food from an extravagant buffet and watching the main table like socially hungry hawks.

Lexi was used to being on display—maybe not exactly like this, but she'd been a performer in many different contexts, both as a Kitty Cat and a gymnast, so she knew she could tune out the gawkers if she needed to. For now, though, she was watching them right back. Figuring out the dynamics, the quiet hierarchy, the frowns and the fake smiles… There wasn't a single person who didn't care. No one was indifferent as to whether or not they were seated at the coveted table.

Sam wasn't at the table, but neither were the two men he'd been chatting with. Lexi assumed the two men were the leaders of the Highwaymen and the Riders. She would have loved to get in on that conversation but had to be satisfied by doing her own recon. She and Sam would share notes later.

"Lexi, baby, how's your back?" Devon said this loud enough for the entire table to hear. Conversations halted and eyes turned.

Lexi was completely taken off guard and suddenly did feel like she was the only one on display. She plastered a smile on her face, forcing herself to look amused. "Oh, you know, broken." She flipped up her hand as if to say, 'no big deal'.

"Oh, darling, so the rumors are true then?" Devon exaggerated a pout. "Your performance days are over? And not even a Kitty Cat any longer either?"

"Yep, all done with that life." She swept the table with her smile. "I'm just a regular girl now." People laughed along with her.

"Oh no, there's nothing regular about you, Lexi." Devon picked up her hand and petted her in long, soft strokes. "Lexi is my very special guest tonight, everyone. She's just retired from a distinguished career and I want to celebrate her right now." He raised his glass in a toast. "To Lexi Monroe, the sexiest woman alive."

Lexi's cheeks hurt from her forced smile, but she picked up her water glass and clinked with Devon. "Thank you. That's very sweet," she said before taking a sip.

"Water?" Devon snapped his fingers at a nearby server. "Please bring Ms. Monroe a proper drink. Why isn't her wineglass filled, at least?" he barked.

Lexi waved the demand away and put her hand on Devon's arm. "I'm fine. Thank you."

"But you're completely sober, darling!" Devon's voice was obnoxiously loud. "You need to catch up with the booze. Bring over a bottle of Champagne!"

Lexi sighed. There'd be no convincing Devon, so it was better for her to go along with his ridiculousness for now.

Within a minute, her flute was full and Devon clinked her glass. "Drink up!"

Lexi took a small sip before putting her glass back down. Devon didn't seem to notice as he downed his own glass in a few gulps. He wiped his mouth with his napkin then leaned in closely to her. "So, tell me. Are you upset about leaving the Kitty Cats?" His breath was a mix of booze and garbage can. She did her best not to gag.

Lexi wanted to move back but had nowhere to go. "It was time to move on." She glanced around and noted that most people had returned to their own conversations.

"Because of your injuries?"

"Partly."

"And was Sabine angry with you for retiring? I mean, I heard her speech at your party. It seemed a little over the top, don't you think?"

It had been the most wonderful speech Lexi had ever heard. It had not only been a catalog of all the accomplishments that Lexi had achieved in both her gymnastics and Kitty Cat worlds, but it had been filled with love and compassion and the genuine sorrow that

Sabine had felt at Lexi leaving the Cowan clan. "Sabine does like to express herself." It physically pained Lexi to insinuate that Sabine had been anything but sincere, but Lexi had to keep her head in this particular game.

"Indeed she does." Devon took another gulp of his newly refilled glass. "Sabine's bodyguard, Adam... He lives in Montana now, doesn't he?"

"He splits his time between New York and Montana, yes." Lexi shifted back a bit as a plate loaded with salad and garlic bread crostini was placed in front of her.

"And he's there now?" Devon picked up his fork.

"He left the night of my retirement party, actually." After he'd said goodbye and had reminded Lexi that he was always only a phone call away, whether she officially worked for Cowan Enterprises or not. Since she knew where Devon was headed in his line of questioning, she added, "He'll be there for three months."

"Oh? Interesting! He's the mastermind behind the security system that protects Sabine's extensive database, right?" He covered his mouth as if he'd let out a big secret. "Oh, I probably shouldn't have said that, right? Sabine's database is confidential, isn't it?"

"What database?" Lexi smiled, hoping to come off as maybe dumb—but also maybe playing dumb.

"Oh, come on, Lexi. Everyone knows that Sabine is harboring some pretty wicked secrets." Devon rolled his eyes. He pointed his fork at her. "Don't play coy with me."

"Yes, you're right. Sabine has trained all her Kitty Cats not only in the art of pleasure but also espionage." She made her tone sound incredulous then forked up some salad and put it in her mouth, all the while looking at Devon like he was crazy.

Devon studied her as though he were trying to figure out if she was mocking him or being honest. "So she doesn't collect information about the men, her clients, who partake in the Kitty Cat amenities?"

Lexi cocked an eyebrow and continued eating.

"Come on, Lexi. Give me something here." He leaned in a little closer. "Inquiring minds want to know."

"Well, Devon." Lexi put her fork down and turned to face him. "I'm sure she wouldn't have a file on you." And that was the truth. Sabine couldn't care less about Devon Caldone. There were no mysteries in his world that she had ever been interested in obtaining…maybe until now, that was.

Devon leaned back, looking a little shocked. Was he supposed to be offended or relieved? She could tell that he really wasn't sure.

"Why all the questions about Sabine? Are you thinking about ending your exclusive membership?" Lexi picked up a crostini and took a bite. "Because you're one of only five hundred men in the top tier. You know that, right?" Devon spent millions to get what he thought was an all-access pass to the Kitty Cat world. "And with a hundred thousand men vying for a place, I would think you'd want to hold on to that perk."

"No, no, are you kidding?" He paused before leaning in once again. "I've been trying to speak with her for a while now, and she's always very preoccupied."

"She's a busy woman."

"Yes, that I know." He laughed awkwardly. "I was wondering if maybe she had something against me? Like maybe my money is good enough for her, but not my company." There was a tinge of anger underlying Devon's words—but also a hint of self-pity.

Lexi proceeded cautiously, because she knew that Devon's fragile ego was something to be mindful of. "You know that's not true. Sabine values your membership. She just doesn't have time for meetings, especially during events."

Devon nodded. "Yes, well, that's the problem. I've attempted to make contact outside of the events, but Adam always seems to intervene. So, I'm wondering, maybe there's something in the database about me that has created some kind of misunderstanding."

Lexi frowned. Was this really about Devon's bruised ego—or something more? It was hard for Lexi to believe that Devon could be that cunning, trying to trick his way into the database by pretending to be worried about Sabine's opinion of him. She had a feeling that he didn't really give a shit about what Sabine thought of him. "And you want me to check for you?"

"Would you?" He patted her hand. "Would you do that for me, Lexi? I'd be eternally grateful if you'd check her database and let me know... I mean, you can use my laptop on the yacht. Or here, use my phone."

"This is all assuming there is a database." Lexi ignored his phone. "And assuming that I had access to that database."

"You? Lexi Monroe? You're one of Sabine's most beloved Kitty Cats," he gushed. "Of course you'd have access, and we both know that a database exists. So, the question is, do you like money?"

Lexi smiled. "Of course... What Kitty Cat doesn't?"

"I happen to have a lot of money, Lexi. A lot." He touched her hand again. "And I'm very willing to give you a substantial retirement trust if you could take a peek into that database and let me know…"

"If there's some dark mark on your name?" Lexi wiped her mouth with her napkin.

"Yes! Exactly!"

"How much money are we talking about here?"

"Five hundred thousand." Devon's expression was deadpan for exactly two seconds before he burst out laughing. "I'm just yanking your chain, baby! How does one-point-five mil sound?"

"Sounds like a lot of money."

"Plus this mansion." He waved his hands around. "Do you like this place? I'll buy it for you. Or any of the other mansions you like in this community. I know the real estate agent handling the sales. I'll make a call." He picked up his phone like he was actually going to call his real-estate-agent friend.

Lexi put her hand on his to stop the call. "This house is beautiful, and your offer is very generous. Let me talk to Samuel about it."

Devon obviously wasn't expecting her to say that, and his eyes nearly bugged out of his head, but he recovered quickly. "Yeah, sure, of course. You need to speak to your man. I get that."

Chapter Ten

"I got something!" both Sam and Lexi said at the same time as soon as they ran into each other.

Sam was coming out of a long corridor where he'd been meeting for the last two hours with Dax and Vince, and Lexi was walking briskly toward him, as if she'd known he was going to turn that corner at that moment.

They gripped each other's arms and Sam felt the vibration of excitement running through Lexi, if only because it matched his own.

Before either one of them could utter another word, Lexi's eyes flashed with lust, again mirroring Sam's feelings exactly, then they were kissing — passionately kissing, gawkers be damned. Sam, desperate for release and pumped up from the meeting he'd just had, maneuvered them back down the corridor. He'd fuck her against the corridor wall if she'd let him, but her mind was obviously working more strategically and she somehow managed to open a door without even breaking their kiss. It was dark, and it was empty. Sam didn't care if there was furniture in there or not. He was totally on board.

"Sam," Lexi gasped, but she was still kissing him.

He pushed her back against the wall and she yelped, then reached behind her and flicked on the light. Sam was blinded for a moment.

"Well, this is…uh…interesting." Lexi laughed.

Sam shifted so he could survey the room. Mirrors. Everywhere. Mirrors mounted on the walls, propped up on the tables, all different shapes and sizes, all giving Sam a view of him and Lexi. He shifted his eyes to hers and grinned. "I guess we'll know what we look like fucking. If we're curious, that is."

"I'm always curious." She winked and pulled him toward her once again, angling her lips so she could kiss him, roving her hands up the front of his shirt, unbuttoning him as she went.

He slipped his hands to her hips and tugged her dress up before sliding his hand over her panty-less pussy. *Mmmmm, yes… I need this woman in my life at all times.* Sex and success went hand in hand for Sam, and when he hit on a big story, like he had tonight, he needed a release, fast and furious.

She was slick and hot. They both groaned when he glided his fingers over her pussy then circled her clit.

"I want it hard, Sam," she moaned. "Fuck me without mercy."

"As you wish," Sam growled.

She was already unzipping his pants, and his cock was so hard that one would think he hadn't just fucked her brains out all day. He grabbed a condom from his pocket. She took it from his hand, opened it then slid it over his aching dick.

She leaned in and pressed her body into his, her lips against his ear. "Fuck me like you mean it," she said, her voice husky with need.

He pushed her, hard, her back thudding against the wall before he yanked her dress up and over her hips. She lifted her leg and he angled her, holding her in place as he slid his cock home — one thrust to get his dick wet, to encase himself deeply and give her a second to adjust. She rolled her hips and he pulled out almost to the tip before slamming her hard, then pumping her fast. He shifted one hand down her leg so he could grip her ass and pull her closer. He squeezed her breast roughly with his other hand while he nipped and licked her neck.

She had her hands on his ass, pulling him into her as she shifted her hips up to meet his urgent thrusts. He was pumping her with everything he had, relentless in his pounding. Her pussy was a quivering wave of spasms, gripping him tightly, a soft, wet cushion of heat.

They were animals, biting and licking, groaning and growling at one another. He needed to feel her, to smell her, to make her scream. He'd landed the story of a lifetime and every nerve ending in his body was fired up, high on adrenaline and lust.

He caught sight of himself in a mirror and felt a surge of triumph to be fucking such a stunningly gorgeous creature. They looked good together, darkness and light, both of them damaged, both of them hungry for release.

His orgasm rose like a freight train, unstoppable and powerful. Lexi cried out, her pussy spasming hard. Sam continued to pummel her, stroking her harder and faster so his climax exploded at the same time hers did.

She clung to him, her arms around his shoulders, gasping with each shudder of her orgasm.

They were both panting. Lexi's fair skin was flushed with color, her freckles popping, her cheeks red and her eyes bright.

Sam kissed her — tender, maybe even forbidden. He was filled with emotion. He wanted to keep Lexi. She slaked his needs in every way. In his sex-fueled high, he thought maybe, *maybe* it would be possible to let her into his fucked-up world, to give her access to his damaged soul. She was so much of everything he loved. He shifted back so he could look into her eyes. She was beautiful, vulnerable and so very fucking strong. He admired her. He desired her more and more every time they fucked. His appetite for redheads aside, wanting Lexi was an unquenchable thirst and Sam was dangerously close to becoming addicted. He pulled out of her, mourning the loss of her heat.

"I've got a lead." The excited rush of landing on something dangerously juicy spiked his adrenaline all over again. "As expected, the Highwaymen and the Riders want a meeting with my father. They know he recently invested in a film company." He helped Lexi straighten her clothes before yanking off the condom. He dropped it into a trashcan then fixed his own pants, righting himself so he looked respectable once again.

"Porn, right? In Germany?" Lexi helped smooth out his shirt. "I overheard Devon at the party last night."

Sam knew she'd been across the room when Devon had started yapping about Sam's dad's recent purchase. He hadn't thought she was listening because she'd appeared to be deep in conversation with her Kitty Cats. Another reason to keep her in his life… They made a good team.

"Yeah, and they think they can get him to fund a project by offering him first dibs on something they know he wants."

"What's that?"

"New York."

Her expression was full of confusion.

"They're going to offer him the smut industry in New York. It's a foothold into territory he wants access to."

"Sabine's territory." Lexi gasped. "These Highwaymen and Riders are going after Sabine."

"They have a plan to dismantle her from the inside out."

"I have to tell Adam!"

"You can't tell Adam! Or anyone. Not yet."

Lexi froze under his grip.

"You need to give me some time, Lexi. Please." His mind was reeling. "I don't know all the details yet. I'm supposed to meet with them again, once I get assurances from my father. I promise, though, there's no immediate danger to Cowan Enterprises, because they admitted that they can't access Sabine's network. They haven't figured out how to get past her online security. It's that good."

She seemed to relax a bit.

"That's why they need an intro to my father, to get access to funds so they can hire this hacker who—"

"A hacker! Sam!"

"Lexi, I swear, I won't let them go that far. I need a day, maybe two, and that's it. Then we can warn Sabine."

"You're going to call your father? Get them the money?"

"Yes." It was a split-second decision, but he wanted this story so badly that he'd be willing to at least dangle the possibility of a meeting with his father.

"Even though you said yourself that you hate the shit your family does?"

"I won't let it go that far. I'll expose the plan, and the Highwaymen and the Riders will go down."

"Even your family?" Lexi gave him a pointed look. "Your family would go down too, wouldn't they?"

That gave him pause. Was he willing to tangle his family in this if it meant they might get arrested—or at least be implicated in everything?

Lexi didn't give him a chance to answer before adding, "You're gambling with everything Sabine has worked her entire life to achieve."

And yet…he couldn't stop this even if he'd wanted to. The plan was in motion already, and he was going along for the ride. He had enough information to start one hell of a story too, but he needed more. "I have it under control. I promise." He put his hands on her arms and gave her a look that he hoped was convincing. "I'm asking for two days. I promise I won't let it go that far."

Lexi stared at him and he wished he could see inside her head, to know what she was thinking, because he couldn't read her expression. Did she trust him enough to let him run with it?

"I'll give you one day, then I'm calling Adam."

"Twenty-four hours?"

She nodded stiffly.

"Okay, deal." He could work with twenty-four hours. He entwined his fingers with hers then started for the door. "I have to think about how to approach this with my father. Maybe you're right. Maybe that's not the way—"

"Devon offered me one-point-five million," Lexi said, "and this mansion, for access to Sabine."

Sam froze and turned to look at her. He couldn't keep the shock from his face. "That's…um…generous. What does he want you to do?"

Is she blushing? It was hard to tell because she was still showing the effects of their fuck.

Her cheeks were flushed with pink and her eyes bright. "He thinks she has a database. He wants to know if he's in it."

"Does she?"

Lexi bit her lip. He could tell that she didn't want to answer.

"Never mind." He pulled back from her. Here he was sharing everything he knew, expecting the same, and yet she had secrets she wasn't willing to share. That was like a kick to the balls.

"I made a promise to you not to tell Sabine about your actual identity. You never made any promises for secrecy to me, and I'm not foolish enough to think you would."

He gulped, feeling gutted that she was probably right. "I always protect my sources."

She looked at him like he'd just confirmed he was as serial killer. "And I always keep my promises."

"Fair enough." Sam couldn't help but feel like this was some kind of betrayal, though.

"What Devon wants and what the Highwaymen and Riders want are connected," Lexi said, reaching for his hand again.

"We have no proof of that."

"Sam."

"Fine, they're connected, of course. How would you access this database?" He raised his hand. "Alleged database."

She rolled her eyes. "Devon insisted I access it from his laptop. He even offered me his phone."

"Right… Probably another attempt to infiltrate Sabine's security. The Highwaymen might have some kind of malware ready to go if the right account is logged into on the right computer or smartphone."

Lexi nodded but didn't speak.

"We have to play this game a little longer, Lexi. I know you're uncomfortable and worried for Sabine, but she's my friend too. I won't let this go too far." Would he sacrifice Sabine for a killer story?

Yes.

No!

Maybe.

Fuck.

"Not even for a good story?" She knew. Of course she knew.

He'd do a lot for a good story. He'd take a lot of risks—push things to the brink, even at great expense. If he thought he could get a little bit closer to the truth, he'd keep going, sometimes to his detriment. It was what made him cutting edge. It kept him ahead of his competition. It ensured that editors reached out to him first. And anything to do with Sabine was pure gold. Every story he'd ever written about her had always gone to a bidding war.

He didn't need the money—he had a trust fund for that—but he loved the glory. It was what made him the reporter he was—the chase, the success, the triumph of unearthing information no one else knew. The praise…

The controversy… He loved it all. It gave him power in its own way.

He'd made a name for himself over the years, and his own family had no idea that he was the hard-hitting reporter that they bitched about publicly. One of his cousins had even made threats against him on his social media. Sam liked to think that his father feared the kind of article Sam Henderson could write about the Dove family.

No one in his family had seen him in the last five years. He'd evaded them in every way possible. He didn't allow pictures to be taken of him. There was no head shot attached to any of his articles. His family had no idea that the clean cut, preppy-looking boy they'd used to know was the tattooed, long-haired, bearded dude whose existence made them so uncomfortable. And that, *that* was the best kind of power Sam could ever hope to achieve over his family. The secret kind of power that was so fucking addictive.

He couldn't stop now, but Lexi was right. There was a lot at risk if he involved his father in this deal.

"Keep playing the game, Lexi. It's too early to quit, and we don't have enough evidence to do anything yet. I'll work my angle and you work yours. Tell Devon you accept his offer."

She opened her mouth as if to argue but he stopped her.

He leaned in and kissed her. "I promise you that we'll both get what we want out of this and no one will get hurt."

He believed what he was telling her. *That counts for something, right?*

Chapter Eleven

Lexi wasn't one hundred percent on board with Sam, but she was close. She was willing to let things play out, if only because she believed in Sam — maybe not enough to betray Sabine's trust but enough to let him lead in whatever way he saw fit...for now.

It concerned her that he was even thinking about getting his father involved in this situation. From what she knew about the notorious Mr. Dove, he was ruthless and cunning, and once he settled on a target, that person paid. What she knew was based on media accounts, however, and Sam had indicated that things weren't as they seemed with his family. Still, she didn't want Sabine to get caught up in the crossfire.

Lexi stepped out of the room with Sam, and they walked down the corridor toward the noise of the party. She looked down at her hands and the nauseating feeling of panic washed through her. "My purse!" She backtracked to the room they'd just been in. Had she brought her purse with her when she'd gone in search of Sam? She couldn't remember. She'd been so caught up in finding him so she could tell him about the deal Devon had made that she couldn't recall picking up her purse. But she wouldn't have left it behind. Her phone was in there — and her meds.

Sam was right behind her, searching the room for her little clutch.

"It's not here." Sam pointed toward the door. "Did you leave it at the table?"

Oh God. The nausea turned into a lump of lead in her stomach. "I must have." *Stupid. Stupid. Stupid.* "I have to go get it."

"I'm sure it's exactly where you left it." Sam held her hand as they left the room. "I'm going to go outside and make a few preliminary calls, see what I can set up." He was giving off a nervous energy that was making her even more jittery. "Get your purse then meet me out there. We can take a car back to the boat and strategize. I want to put some distance between us and everyone here."

Lexi nodded. She needed time to think too. The music was so loud it was almost impossible to focus. "I'll be quick."

She watched Sam beeline for the front entrance then turned into the next room so she could cut through to the dining room. There were so many people milling around and shouts of laughter, loud talking and music pumping. It was enough to give anyone a headache. Her gaze landed on Devon, who was huddled in the corner with the two men she'd met earlier, Dax and Vince. No one looked happy. In fact, Devon was flinging his arms around like he was trying to gesture his way out of something. Dax, the tall, lanky-looking one, had his finger in Devon's face and was yelling — or at least he looked like he was yelling. Lexi couldn't hear a word of what was being said over the noise of the party. Vince, the burly, rugged one, had his arms crossed and look even more menacing than when she'd first met him.

She didn't know if the argument between the three men had anything to do with her or Sam, but her gut was telling her that whatever was going on was not good for either of them.

The table was still full of people, everyone eating and drinking, talking loudly and not even noticing Lexi at all. She swooped down to search under the table for her purse. It had been shifted from the table leg where she remembered putting it and was now lying in between her chair and Devon's. She was just about to snag it when she felt hands wrap around her waist. She was hauled backward, then flung up like a ragdoll.

She yelped, terrified that she was being abducted or something, then she heard Devon's obnoxious laugh. He pulled her up and cradled her awkwardly in his arms, jarring her body to the side as she landed against him.

"What are you doing?" she gasped, trying for a weak smile but failing miserably. She was off kilter and her body contorted in a way that didn't feel good.

"Oh, just sweeping you off your feet." He nuzzled his face into her neck and murmured, "I saw Samuel leave. Did you two have a spat?"

"What? No!" She wriggled a little, testing to see how strong his grip was.

"Did you talk to the *boss* about my proposal?" He pulled back to look at her and she realized that his pupils were completely blown, open in a drugged-out kind of way. He had an aggressive edge to his voice, which she assumed was a result of the fight she'd witnessed between him and the other men.

"Yes." She put her hand on his chest. "Devon, put me down, please."

He tightened his grip. "Will you accept my offer?" he growled.

She winced, her twisted muscles starting to really strain. "Yes, yes, I will. Of course I will."

"Good decision." Without warning, he dropped her to her feet. She rolled out of his arms and felt her back tweak hard. She landed on her knees. Devon put his hand in her hair and let out a bark of a laugh. "Well, honey, if you wanted to show your appreciation that way, you should have said so."

Everyone was looking at them now. Everyone started to laugh. Lexi burned with rage, but she was in too much pain to do anything about it right now. Her back spasmed. She put her hands on the one Devon had in her hair and dug her nails in until he let her go.

"Now, now, no need to be like that," he snarled.

She reached out a shaky hand and grabbed her purse and realized immediately that something had been taken. Her phone was there, but her pain meds were missing. *Fuck.* Of course, they were.

Devon scooped her up under the arm and helped her to stand. "So sorry, babe. I heard you liked it rough." He leaned in close again. "Did I hurt you?" His tone was so cloying and insincere.

She gulped back the scream of pain that was trapped in her throat and forced herself to smile at him. "I'm not that easy to break." She shook his hand off and walked out of the dining room, using every ounce of inner strength she had not to burst into tears.

Her pain meds were extremely powerful opioids, too tempting for someone to leave behind if they'd been snooping in her purse. She'd been extremely lucky that they hadn't taken her phone as well.

She had more pain meds, of course, but they were on the boat, and it was going to take her at least thirty minutes to get back there so she could take one. Movement was excruciating. Each step she took shot knife-stabbing pain through her spine.

Sam was on the phone, but the second he saw her face as she came out of the house, he hung up and closed the distance between them. "What happened?" He put his arm around her waist, which felt like a vise clamping down.

"Please, d-d-don't," she whimpered, trying her hardest to keep it together. "Can you let me lean on you? Just put your arm around my shoulder." She somehow managed to stretch her arm around his waist to make it look like they were cuddling as they walked toward one of the waiting cars.

"What happened, Lexi?" His voice was low, too low for anyone else to hear.

"I twisted my back." She didn't want to tell him what had happened. It was humiliating enough that at least a dozen people had seen it go down. Devon had been asserting his dominance and it was meant to send a message, to her, to Sam and to everyone who'd witnessed it. "Devon picked me up then let me fall."

Sam tensed. She knew he wanted to go back to the party so he could deal with Devon, but instead, he said, "What do you need me do?"

She wanted to say, *Go punch his lights out!* She wanted to say, *Humiliate that asshole in front of his guests!*

"Can you take me to our cabin, please? I have pain meds there."

"I thought you brought some with you." He took her purse from her hand.

"S-s-someone…" She gulped back another yelp as her back pulled. "Someone took them out of my purse."

"Fuck!" Sam got them to the last car on the driveway and helped her slide into the back seat. "Get us back to the yacht, double time," he said once he'd seated himself, then slammed the door closed. "What's the best way for you to sit? Do you want to lie down with your feet propped up?"

Lexi was bracing herself for the inevitable bumps in the road that would jar her spasming muscles more. She shook her head. "I'm okay like this." 'Okay' was not exactly what was going on, but at least she could try to move with the turns and anticipate the stops and starts. It was going to be a long ride back to the boat.

"Why did Devon do that? Was he showing off or something?"

"I don't think he meant to hurt me, not exactly. I think he forgot about my injury or maybe didn't think about it. He was angry…" She hissed in a breath when the car made a sharp turn onto another street. "After you walked away, I saw Devon and those other two guys, Dax and Vince. They were arguing. Dax looked like he was threatening Devon. They didn't care who saw them, either. They were in the corner of a room, but there were lots of people around." She put her hand on the door as they took another turn. "He was pissed off and looking for someone to bully." As she said those words, it crossed her mind that maybe Devon *had* intended to hurt her. Maybe he'd known exactly what he was doing all along and she had underestimated him this whole time.

"That son of a bitch!" Sam ran his hand through his hair, yanking away the tie and letting the waves fall around his face. "That's what that asshole does. I've seen it a million times. Embarrass him in some way and he tries to save face, pushing around someone, usually a woman, to show how strong he is."

"He wanted to know if I'd made my decision. It was obvious that I didn't really have a choice." She tried to turn toward Sam but settled for a shifting her head slightly. "Something went down between those guys. Something has changed."

"We should get our stuff and leave. Head back to Miami. Forget this investigation."

"No." Lexi shook her head. "We can't stop now. I need to know what's happening so I can help Sabine. I need evidence."

"Lexi—"

"No, Sam, you said it before. We need to keep playing this game. We need to find out what's going on."

He was quiet for a few minutes, and when he finally spoke, his voice was low. "I'm not going to lie. I want this story."

"I know."

He took her hand. "I've got a plan."

She gulped, nodded and tried to steady herself without wincing. "I'm in. Whatever it is. I'm in."

Chapter Twelve

As long as Lexi didn't move, she could manage the muscle spasms. That was a problem, of course, as soon as they pulled up to the marina.

"I can carry you," Sam offered.

She so badly wanted him to, but she didn't want anyone to see that, even if it was only the yacht staff. Eventually, that information would get back to Devon — and she would rather die than let him know he'd hurt her.

"It's probably better if I move." Which wasn't a total lie. She'd learned the hard way during recovery that the more she lay around, the more her muscles froze, which only made the pain that much worse when she did start moving.

She shifted gingerly, though, making sure she wasn't tweaking her back the wrong way and aggravating the problem as she slipped out of the car. Sam moved at her pace, his hand resting lightly on her hip, letting her use him for support as she walked without it looking like that was what she was doing.

The staff was busy getting the yacht up to Devon's standards and didn't bother with Lexi and Sam, other than to check that they didn't need anything. The second they were in their cabin, Lexi headed for the bed and Sam headed for her luggage.

"Side pocket." Lexi gritted her teeth as she eased herself onto the mattress.

Sam came with a glass of water and her pill bottle.

"Could you fish one out for me?" She took the glass.

"Only one?" He frowned but did as she asked.

"I just need to take the edge off. I don't want to drool." She attempted a laugh, but it came out as a cough.

"You know what's best." Sam sat down next to her. "Would a massage help?"

She was mid swallow and nearly choked. The image of Sam massaging her naked body flashed through her mind, and that did amazing things for her mood.

"I'm pretty good with my hands."

"That I know." She handed him the glass. "A massage would be nice. Maybe not right around my scar though."

Sam rubbed his hands together. "Roll over."

She laughed. "Unzip me and I will."

Sam locked eyes with her, probably checking to see if her tone matched her expression. Once her pain meds kicked in, she'd be looking for a little sexual distraction, especially if it came with some pain. *Does that make me weird? That I crave the kind of pain Sam can give me? If it does, I don't care.*

She motioned to her back. "Isn't it better if I'm naked?"

He nodded. "Always." He helped her unzip.

She moved slowly, letting her dress slip from her shoulders. Sam tugged it over her breasts and down to her waist. His breath grew heavy as he supported her so she could stand and shimmy the dress over her hips until it pooled at her feet. She stepped out of it slowly then moved back to the bed. If he was feeling apprehensive about anything sexual happening between them, seeing her naked seemed to be eliminating that very quickly, exactly as she'd planned. She wanted him primed and ready to fuck her brains out as soon as the pill started to work.

One pill wouldn't help a lot, but she was counting on another round of bondage, maybe some spanking, nipple tweaking, whatever he could give her. First, she needed to wear down his defenses and get him to set aside his concern for her wellbeing enough to want to give her a dose of pain.

"You okay if I run to the closet?" He was hovering, clearly torn between wanting to help but not wanting to smother her. She appreciated that, but she needed him in another mood altogether if she was going to get any relief.

"I'm good. It's not that bad," she lied with a smile on her face.

Sam nodded. "Shout if you need me." He bolted for the closet.

She gritted her teeth and crawled forward, going at a sloth-like speed until she could lower herself down to her stomach. She instantly felt some relief — the throbbing eased to more of a drumbeat rather than a punching stab.

Sam came out of the closet with a small bottle in his hand. "Knew this would come in handy someday.

Massage oil for emergencies. Keep it in my duffel." He laughed.

She laughed too—or tried to, anyway. "You're very prepared."

"Condoms and massage oil—the perfect seduction plan." He winked then climbed onto the bed, being careful in his movements. "You let me know if I'm hurting you."

"A little pain isn't going to kill me," she reminded him.

Sam dripped some of the oil between her shoulder blades. It smelled like mint and something clovey. He rubbed his hands together again before pressing his fingers onto her muscles. He was gentle at first, tracing the line of her shoulders, down her spine, stopping well before he got to her scar, then going back up again.

She sighed. Gentle was nice. It might put her to sleep, but it was good. It made her mind start to wander to the pleasurable things she'd been denying herself since the accident. She didn't like anyone seeing the damage to her body. She didn't like to show weakness in any way, and that made her seem cold, less inviting. That was part of the problem with trying to resume her career as a Kitty Cat. Clients expected her to be transparent with them—or at least to make them think she was an open book. If they knew about her accident, they wanted the story, and once they heard it—or at least the version she told them—they wanted to baby her, to pity her.

It had been a vicious cycle for Lexi, and it had sent her into a depression as she slowly began to realize that things could never really be as they had been. Any time someone had touched her she'd flinched, even her regular customers. That was how it had started to fall apart. She hadn't wanted those tender touches. She hadn't wanted their pity. Under normal circumstances and pre-accident, clients had wanted to pretend she was their girl. They'd wanted to take care of her, pamper her, treat her like an object, and she couldn't let her guard down enough to do that anymore or even pretend that she could tolerate it. The joy she'd once gotten from all the role play and pretending was gone. It wasn't just her back that had broken that day on the beam. It was her. She'd broken. And the pieces that had been put back together were all wrong.

It was overwhelming to realize that Sam was touching her so gently and she wasn't flinching away. She wasn't feeling that impulse to ask him to stop, either.

"Is this okay?"

She gulped back the emotion she felt, knowing that Sam had somehow broken through her defenses without her even realizing it. "I haven't let anyone touch me like this in a very long time. Other than my various therapists, no one has seen my scar either."

Sam stayed quiet, maybe sensing that she needed to talk her way through the emotions welling up.

"I had this coach" — her voice caught a little — "a new guy who came highly recommended. Claude LePele. He convinced my manager that we'd be able to go further…to the Olympics, even though I was well past the age that it was even logical. I wanted it so badly, though. We'd been together for a few months. He was tough, a hard trainer. I liked it. It made me feel more competitive, like I had an edge that the other gymnasts didn't."

Sam dug in a bit more, working the lines of her muscles with his thumbs, making her feel the knots she hadn't even realized she had across her shoulders. She hissed when he hit a particularly bad one.

"Too much?" he said, but he didn't pause.

"Never." She breathed through his movements as he kneaded her muscles with his knuckles. God, she loved the euphoria that came with Sam's version of pain. He was digging into her back now, really working out the kinks.

"So, he was a good coach then?"

Lexi swallowed the bitter laugh that bubbled up. "He was abusive. I didn't really see it. I ignored my manager's warnings when she started to hear things, bad things, about him. But Claude and I got along when we weren't training, so I chalked it up to disgruntled gymnasts who weren't hungry enough for a win. He had me working this new routine on the beam. It was aggressive and dangerous. I loved it. I knew if I could pull it off, it would get me top scores. I trained so hard. Then one day, Claude was in an awful mood. He was ranting about things that were wrong with the system, with the government, with the world. I suspected he'd been drinking but went ahead with training anyway. I was used to his loud voice and criticism, so I just did what I normally do, tune out the negative and concentrate on my routine. Except, I wasn't paying attention to what he was doing." Lexi paused because the memory of what had happened flashed so vividly that it took her breath away.

"You don't have to tell me—"

But she did. She did have to tell him—and that scared the hell out of her. Letting him into her world came with consequences for her and her tender heart. "I jumped into the splits. A simple move to put me in position for a more complicated one. As I was in the air,

Claude shouted something, and when I came down, the beam wasn't where it was supposed to be." She gulped back the memory of the shock she'd felt. *The beam wasn't there*. It should have been right where she'd left it. "It was only a fraction of an inch to the left, enough of a distance to make me land all wrong. My foot slipped. I hit my spine." She didn't actually remember any of that—her hitting the beam then hitting the floor, her back splitting open from connecting the beam's edge so hard, blood everywhere, people rushing to her, the paramedics arriving. She remembered none of it. "I couldn't move my legs at first. The doctors in the ER thought I was paralyzed, but it turned out to be a compression fracture."

"Surgery fixed things?"

"Yes. There's nerve damage. That's what mainly causes my pain. My muscles are seriously fucked up down there, prone to tweaking the wrong way. I carry a lot of tension, which makes matters worse."

Sam was quiet again, working his way over her ribs.

"Everyone thought it was a terrible accident until they'd watched the video." One of the other gymnast's coaches had been taping Lexi, trying to figure out how to compete. He'd caught the entire thing. "Claude moved the beam," Lexi said. It still hurt her to think about it. Even though they'd only been together for a few months, it had been six to eight hours a day of working together for all those months. They'd eaten meals together. They'd shared stories—funny ones, sad ones. She'd trusted him. "He'd shouted for me to expect the unexpected, then had moved the beam."

"Holy fuck!" Sam stopped massaging her. "Are you fucking serious?"

She liked his anger. She liked that he was feeling rage on her behalf—not pity. Rage. "I watched it happen on the video."

"Is that why there was a media blackout?" Sam put his hands back on her body. "Is that why no one knows what actually happened? Is this Claude asshole being protected?"

Yes. "No. He was stripped of his coaching credentials and has been banned from all training facilities in the United States."

"That son of a bitch. That's all he got?"

"I sued him and he settled." He didn't want to be known as the man who'd sabotaged Lexi Monroe's career with one careless action. "He paid dearly." *One-point-two million, to be exact.* His insurance had paid some of it, but the rest was on him. It'd wiped him out financially. Last she'd heard, he'd moved out of the country.

"You paid dearly too." Sam sighed and Lexi waited for the inevitable pity that was coming. She was, after all, pitiful.

"It was the gymnastics association that demanded my silence." They'd muzzled her, had treated her not as the victim but as someone who'd been careless and who'd be inconsiderate if she were willing to go against her fellow gymnasts. The truth would tarnish the brand of the National Gymnastics League—and they couldn't have that.

He dug his thumbs back into the knot he'd found earlier, sending a thud of delicious pain straight to her core. Okay, maybe he wasn't pitying her. Maybe he was going to give her exactly what she needed. He didn't relent. Even when she squirmed, he just kept working the stubborn knot.

"You lost everything you loved because of what happened."

"Yes." The truth of that still made her heart constrict.

"You loved working for Sabine."

Lexi nodded. "I loved being a Kitty Cat. It was so thrilling to be the center of attention like that, to be so valued by Sabine and looked up to by the other Cats. I had made a name for myself."

"But the accident ruined it all."

She gulped. It had. "I have demons."

"Darkness," Sam said, like he knew exactly what she meant. "It pulls you under."

"Yes."

He dug his fingers harder into her muscles. "You're drowning."

"Until I met you." It took a lot to admit that to him, but it was true. Sam understood her darkness. He knew what she needed, when she needed it.

He was quiet for a long time, rubbing her back.

"Sam, I only told you because—"

"What do you want from me, Lexi?" His voice was gravelly, his fingers still working her muscles.

Lexi shivered. "You know what I want." *What I need.*

The pain in her lower back was nothing but a dull beat, the pain meds having finally kicked in.

Sam stopped massaging her. He got up. She was about to look over her shoulder when he yanked on her ankles, pulling her suddenly to the edge then half off the bed. Her feet were planted on the floor, her arms above her head. She heard the snap of his belt seconds before she felt the bite of it on her ass.

She whimpered, then moaned. He struck her thighs. *Whack. Whack.* Then back up to her ass. *Whack. Whack.* Each hit was wicked sharp and unrelenting and brought her deep emotional pain to the surface. Her skin burned. Her muscles in her ass ached. She bit her bottom lip to keep from crying out. Pulses of pleasure rolled up and down her body and she forgot about her back pain. All her focus was on the belt meeting her flesh. This sweet pain was what she'd asked for. It was pain that she controlled. One word and Sam would stop.

Just when she thought she couldn't take another hit, Sam was on his knees, spreading her legs, opening her up from behind. She couldn't see him, only feel him, his warm breath panting against her hot, wet pussy. He rubbed her asshole with the fingers of one hand and slipped his other into her pussy. She jolted when the tip of his thumb pressed into her ass and zinged when he found her clit. He rubbed, flicked and licked. She arched back, writhing as her orgasm started to rise. It was hard and fast, like a giant explosion of release that she so badly needed. Adrenaline flooded through her, making her whole body hum.

Sam moved away. She looked over her shoulder, dizzy from her climax, but he'd changed position. He'd stood then tugged on her arms, wrapping the belt around her wrists and tightening until she winced. He put the necktie he'd used earlier around her eyes, then, much to her surprise, stuck earplugs into each of her ears.

It was almost complete sensory deprivation. Sound was muffled. Her own breathing sounded too loud. He turned her around and helped her off the bed. The carpet was plush beneath her feet. The air in the room was cool but comfortable. She thought he was walking her to the closet again, but when her feet touched cold tile, she knew the bathroom was their next destination.

He pulled her arms up, stretching her almost on tiptoe, and moved her backward until the door closed. Suddenly he was gone and she was suspended from the door, up on tiptoes, her arms straining from having to hold up her own weight.

Sound came in a muffled way. He hadn't left her alone. She could kind of hear him moving around, doing stuff. Excitement burned through her, beating to the same tempo as the welts on her ass from his belt. Her pussy was slick. She wanted him to fuck her senseless.

She felt the steam rise around her and realized he must have turned on the shower. Goosebumps rose all over her skin as the heat of the bathroom caressed her, coating her. She breathed it in, smelled soap mixed with hot air. It swirled around her body and invaded her lungs.

The sensation of his mouth on her nipple jolted her. He licked her once on each one then disappeared again. She wanted his hands on her — his dick in her.

He rubbed something over her nipples this time, circling, circling...and suddenly she felt the slow burn start there and smelled the distinct scent of toothpaste. "Ohhhh," she moaned. *Toothpaste, very clever.* The longer it stayed on, the warmer it would get, and by the feel of things, Sam was pouring it on really good.

He left again and she strained to hear what he was up to. Her nipples were tingling, growing warmer, her ass still smarting and the heat of the steam rising around her made her body feel loose, wobbly, relaxed — a contrast to everything else. She couldn't see and she couldn't really hear, so the sensations of everything else were heightened.

Sam came back, this time with a warm, wet washcloth. He rubbed along her ribs gently, tickling her with the light touch, then moved over her hip, then across her thigh until…until…she moaned. He used the wet cloth to stroke her clit, abrading her with its texture.

All the sensations on her skin swirled together. Her nipples burned, her skin was hot from the steam and the cloth Sam was using to rub her clit felt rougher by the second.

It was everything she needed. There was so much to feel, so much to savor. Her body vibrated and her arms shook. When he pulled away suddenly, she cried out, her own voice sounding hollow in her head.

Something cold touched her hot nipples and she flinched away — too much cold against her skin. It was delicious torture as he slowly wiped and wiped, taking the burn of the toothpaste away with each stroke. It took forever. His only touch was on her nipples, soothing her burn, rubbing roughly at the same time, a tantalizing contrast. When he finished, he opened the door, forcing her to move a few steps on tiptoe. Cool air flooded in. He pulled her arms down then pushed her over — bending her at the same time as he was walking her, until her cheek lay flat against the cool, damp marble of the countertop and her hands dangled, still tied together.

He held her hips. She braced herself for his thrust, but instead she felt his hands on her stomach, touching her softly, tracing a pattern over her skin. It lulled her, her muscles relaxing until, in a flash, he clamped onto her nipples, pinching with his fingers, then squeezing her breasts hard with his hands. She cried out at the same time that he pushed inside her, drilling her so forcefully from behind that her cheek skidded across the marble.

Her nipples throbbed, but he didn't let go. He just tightened his grip and rolled the sensitive buds between his thumbs and fingers as he fucked her from behind.

Her orgasm exploded with little warning, spasming around Sam's cock so intensely that she didn't think it would ever end. His climax crested, making his thrusts fiercer, his cock so hard that it was like a lead pipe drilling deep inside her. "Yes, yes, yes!" His voice sounded hoarsely muffled, barely audible as actual words because of the plugs in her ears. It was sexy as hell.

They rocked together for another full minute before Sam released her nipples and pulled out of her still-throbbing pussy.

She had no words. Her body was languid, her back pain obliterated for now. She could curl up in bed and fall asleep.

Except Sam had other plans. He guided her toward the shower, which was still steaming up the room, and helped her in. He untied her hands and removed the earplugs and blindfold, then turned her around and kissed her.

"Let's finish what we started in here," he said.

Chapter Thirteen

Lexi felt good. Her body was loose, easy to maneuver — the tension that had been screaming through her muscles for the last hour was gone. He'd fucked it out of her. But Sam wanted to wash her. He wanted to show her tenderness, not pity, for everything she'd endured. Sharing her story with him was a big deal. He knew that.

It was obvious that she didn't like feeling vulnerable, and she didn't want people to treat her differently. Her bravado all the way from the mansion to the yacht was a testament to her strength, but all the same, Devon shouldn't have laid his hands on her and Sam was going to rip a strip off him when he got back to the yacht. He wasn't trying to be her knight in shining armor. It wasn't about that. Sam didn't like that Devon had been so careless with her body.

Fucking idiot.

Lexi looked confused but went along with him guiding her into the hot shower. She moaned when the water cascaded over her skin and he was certain he'd made the right decision. A hot shower always helped him sleep after a good fuck.

Besides, he'd been fantasizing about washing her for months. It was strange, sure, but everyone had their thing, and Sam loved shower sex and lusted for Lexi's tight body all the damn time.

After he'd stripped off his own clothes then got in with her, he moved her under the spray to wet her hair, which went from lighter red to a deep auburn the wetter it got. He loved redheads, but Lexi's hair was always so silky-looking and it cascaded over her shoulders in bouncy waves when it was dry. Now it was plastered to her pale skin, gaining length as the water weighed it down. He turned her around before grabbing the shampoo.

One of the most sensual things he could think of was washing a woman's hair. He knew from experience that it felt amazing to have a lover do a scalp massage, especially after mind-blowing sex. He worked the shampoo into a lather and piled her hair up so he could get it all. She leaned into him a bit, her body swaying as he used his fingers to rub all over her head. He planned on giving her a massage from top to bottom, and his cock definitely approved. He'd never get enough of this woman, not in a million years.

Once he got the shampoo worked in, he tilted her head back and rinsed it all out, loving how her hair ran through his fingers, the feel of it over his palms making his body tingle in all the right ways. Lexi was one sexy woman all the time, but wet, *oh man*, she was melt-on-the-spot burning.

He wasn't the kind of Neanderthal to forget conditioner. He gobbed it on generously, because he knew how much his own hair needed it, and he repeated the process of massaging her scalp then rinsing it all out.

He grabbed a washcloth and poured some body wash onto it, then used it to massage Lexi's body all over again. He didn't dig into her muscles, though. He was gentle, taking his time to trail along her contours and over her curves. He circled her tits, wiping away any remaining toothpaste. Lexi was breathing hard, her eyes closed. When he reached her pussy, he dropped the washcloth and used his finger to caress her clit. Lexi leaned into him, her head on his shoulder, her arms loose around his waist.

She came quietly, just a whimper and a shudder, then a sigh. Sam kissed the top of her head before turning the water off. As much as he wanted to fuck her again, he knew she was exhausted. His needs could wait.

The room was still filled with steam, so it was warm, but all the same, he grabbed the biggest towel he could find and used it to dry her off before wrapping it around her body. He grabbed a smaller towel for her hair and tried to get as much of the water out as possible.

He dried himself quickly then opened the bathroom door, letting the cool air roll in. Lexi was shivering a little when Sam picked her up, cradling her in his arms as he walked to the bed. She looked like she was half asleep already, so he didn't waste any time getting her under the covers then climbing in after her. Her damp hair was fanned out on her pillow and smelled of strawberries and vanilla. He draped his arm over her waist and curled himself around her.

He could get so used to this. Having Lexi in his arms was fulfilling him in ways that he knew were dangerous. He cupped her breast. She moaned and wiggled back so that they were snug against each other.

Fuck, he wanted so badly to keep her in his world. It made him think hard about what he was planning on doing to get a story out of this fucked-up situation between Devon and the crime bosses. If Sam got his father involved in this, then Lexi would be too close to that world — and that was something Sam didn't want. It would likely ruin what was happening between them, and there was *definitely* something happening between them. At least, Sam felt like there was.

Everything his father had touched in Sam's world had inevitably been destroyed by him, usually when his father's best intensions were involved. That was why Sam had distanced himself all those years ago. He'd made sure that his dad couldn't fuck things up for him anymore. So why was he even considering bringing his father into this situation?

There had to be a way around that — a way to make the Highwaymen and the Riders think that they were getting support from Sam's father without actually bridging that gap.

Sam nuzzled his lips against Lexi's neck. "I'm going to take care of things, Lexi. I'm going to make sure we come out of this on top." She couldn't hear him. Her breathing had deepened and her body was languid. He wrapped his arms around her and let his mind wander to all the ways he'd cherish her if he could just keep her in his life.

Chapter Fourteen

Lexi woke up feeling very good. She was refreshed, satiated beyond belief and hopeful, all thanks to Sam. She allowed herself a good stretch, testing the limits of her back. Things were still sore, but not as bad as they had been after Devon had dropped her.

"What time is it?" Lexi yawned as she reached for her phone on the nightstand. "Sam?" She checked the time. Nine p.m. *Wow!* She'd slept the day away, something she hadn't done in a very long time. Uninterrupted sleep did wonders for her mental state too. She was happy, even though she knew the night would bring some tricky things to navigate.

Sam had been so wonderful in the early hours of the morning. Normally she would have rejected any tenderness for fear of falling into emotions she had no real capacity to follow through on, but after he'd fucked her brains out and had helped her pain management, she'd been open to anything he'd wanted to do. He'd taken her into the shower and had been so considerate.

He'd given her what she'd needed without taking anything more for himself. He'd taken care of her in a way that hadn't felt like pity at all.

She wanted to give him some of that back right now. Lexi craned her neck so she could see into the bathroom, but the lights were off in there, so she moved on the bed to look into the closet.

He was sitting at a makeshift desk, a small table with his laptop on it angled against the wall. He'd dragged a chair in there that really didn't look very comfortable, but he was doing it so that he didn't disturb her while she slept. He had on noise cancelling headphones. She laughed to herself. Right, he couldn't hear her. Lexi slid out of bed, not bothering to take a sheet to cover up. She was going to give him the best ride of his life, right on that chair.

She crept up behind him, not intending to look at this computer screen, but when her gaze landed on the very familiar National Gymnastics League website, she froze. *What the…?*

He caught her reflection in the screen and closed the window before turning around. "Oh, hey." He tugged his headphones off. "How are you feeling?"

Did I see that right? Why is he on that website? Her stomach did a flip—and not in a good way.

He didn't give her a chance to speak, or maybe she was just so caught off guard that she didn't know what to say. Either way, he was up and out of the chair in a flash. He pulled her into his arms and kissed her with such intensity that her mind instantly clouded with lust. The chemistry between them felt that powerful — powerful enough to make her second guess what she thought she'd seen.

"Devon was by here about an hour ago. I told him you'd be ready to meet him at midnight. Is that okay?"

Lexi frowned. "Meet Devon?"

"Yeah, so you can log into the database…or whatever."

"I'm not going to—"

"It's okay. I've got a plan." Sam led her into the bedroom and guided her to a chair. "Hear me out, okay?"

She felt a little weird sitting there naked, but Sam was so wound up that he seemed oblivious to her current state. His eyes were bright, his face a little flushed.

"I've been thinking a lot about what you said…you know, about getting my father involved in this situation." He waved his hands around. "And you're right. Calling my father would be opening a box of snakes with no way of shutting it again."

Had she said that? She remembered being concerned about his father and what could possibly go wrong.

"So, I've made a few calls and I've pulled together enough ready cash to front the Highwaymen's plan myself."

If Lexi's eyes opened any wider with surprise, she'd be worried about her eyeballs falling right out. "How much money are we talking about here?" She figured a lot.

"Five million." He perched himself on the corner of the bed. "I've got a trust."

"You have a trust with five million dollars in it?"

Sam winced. "No." He stood up and starting pacing. "I have a trust worth forty-five million."

Lexi's mouth fell open.

"And I rarely touch it. It's guilt money." He paused and gave a bitter-sounding laugh. "My father set it up for me when I was eighteen."

"If you give the Highwaymen and the Riders your money, they'll have the funds to be able to go after Sabine." Lexi felt more than naked now. She felt exposed. "I really don't think it's a good —"

"Please, hear me out, okay?" He winced. "Do you want a robe?"

She could have laughed that he'd only just realized she was sitting there naked…or maybe she could have cried. Naked Lexi was an after-thought right now. No way would she be distracting him with the state his mind was in. "That would be nice."

He nodded then disappeared into the closet. He was back out within seconds, a white terrycloth robe draped over his arm. "Sorry… I should have gotten this for you sooner."

She slipped the robe over her arms then adjusted herself so she could wrap it around her body and tie it off. It was strange how a piece of material could give a person back a feeling of control. Lexi was comfortable in her nakedness under normal circumstances, but right now things were far from normal.

Sam sat down on the bed again, but he wasn't still. He was tapping his foot to a beat Lexi couldn't hear. "The bank can pull the funds I need in a couple of hours, then I can wire transfer it to a bank of the Highwaymen's choice…if it comes to that."

"What do you mean?"

"I'm going to meet them back at the mansion in an hour."

"You're going to meet with gang leaders at an empty mansion alone?" Lexi shook her head. "Sam —"

"I'm an investigative reporter, Lexi. This is what I do. There's nothing to worry about. Dax and Vince have no reason not to trust me, and I'll be giving them the money they need for their operation."

"When they find out you haven't called your father, they'll likely be pissed off. Don't you think that's part of the plan too? To get that introduction for future deals?"

"My father wouldn't have agreed to that anyway. He doesn't form alliances with men like Dax and Vince. I'll explain that to them. I can even tell them an intro will come later, if this deal works out. I'll tell them that my father will be impressed if they pull it off."

"Making them think this is some kind of trial for them?"

"Exactly." He sighed. "My father is a criminal. He's made an empire off shady shit. I won't deny that or excuse it, but he has limitations — scruples, I guess you could say. His targets have been bad people. He's built an empire on the backs of other criminals and has developed a reputation that is so inflated, thanks to that fucking TV show, that people and other criminals, think he's worse than he is."

Lexi nodded. "If he's such a great guy, why did you exile yourself?"

"I'm the sole heir, Lexi. His only child. He wants me to take over — and I can't do that."

Lexi wasn't the kind of person to hold standards that she wasn't about to meet herself. She'd participated in criminal shit working for Sabine. She'd done things that had crossed a bunch of lines, and maybe that made her a bad person in the eyes of some. Hell, she'd been an escort, for fuck's sake. Society looked at women like her with scorn, even when many of them paid her expensive New York rent with their patronage. "So, you don't want your dad to know what you're up to."

"I don't want him to get tied up with Dax and Vince." He shrugged, and she saw how torn he was. He probably wasn't even sure why he was doing what he was doing, only that he didn't want anyone to get hurt.

Families are complicated.

"Okay, so if Dax and Vince go for this deal of yours and you wire the money, then what happens?"

"I'm only going to wire the money if they go into explicit detail about the plan rather than wash over the details like they did at our meeting earlier. They evaded my probing techniques like pros. Seriously, I felt like a fucking amateur in that room." He shook his head like he was still trying to make sense of how it had all gone down. "I'm going to record the conversation."

"That's illegal in Florida." Lexi knew a thing or two about audio recording without consent. In some states, a person could record a conversation with only one person's consent and that one person could be the person doing the recording. "Florida has a two-party consent law. You'd need permission before you could record them. I mean, if you plan to use it in an article, that is." Lexi had illegally recorded plenty of conversations, but they'd all gone into Sabine's database, to be used at a later date as the need arose. It was amazing how often the threat of extortion got things done without ever having to use the information at hand.

Sam shook his head. "What are they going to do? Sue me? I'm going to get enough information to get them arrested."

"What about retaliation?"

"They won't touch me."

"Because of your father?"

"Yes."

"It sounds too risky, Sam."

"Everything worth something comes with a little risk." Sam shrugged. "Besides, no one knows what Sam Henderson looks like. There are no profile pictures, no pictures on the web. It's an alias that I keep very protected. I've got nothing to lose and everything to gain. This story would be a huge prize to a lot of media outlets, and I'd be exposing some dangerous scum for all to see. They won't be able to hide in the shadows anymore."

"You risk losing five million dollars! Once you transfer that money, it's gone."

"Yeah, but like I said, the money is tainted anyway. The interest on the money I have is absurd. I wouldn't be able to spend it all in a lifetime."

He leaned forward and rested his elbows on his knees, steepling his hands under his chin. "The alternative is too risky. Getting my family involved will create a total shitshow and will likely end up with people getting hurt or killed on all sides." Sam shook his head. "My dad is like a bull in a china shop. He destroys everything he touches because his focus is so intense, and he doesn't understand the meaning of a gentle touch."

"Okay, then I'm coming with you to the meeting."

"No." Sam got up from the bed. "Absolutely not."

"Sam, you can't go alone."

"This is what I do, Lexi. I know how to take risks without getting hurt. Trust me."

She did trust him, but her gut was telling her that something was off. "So I'm supposed to sit in this cabin and worry about you?"

He seemed surprised by her words, like he'd never expect her to worry about him. "You have to give Devon what he wants."

"Uh…nah, no way."

"You have to let Devon *think* you're giving him what he wants." Sam pointed toward his computer. "I created a database. It looks legit, or at least, what my imagination came up with for an alleged database of secrets. You'll have to log in and everything. Devon will think you're giving him what he wants, then you'll leave, get the hell off this boat and meet me at Key West International airport. I've chartered a plane and it'll take off as soon as we're both there."

Lexi was shocked and impressed—but mostly shocked. "What happens if something goes wrong?"

Sam put his hands on her upper arms and helped her stand. He looked right into her eyes, and she was sure that whatever he was going to say next, he believed it one hundred percent. "Nothing will go wrong."

Lexi winced. There was nothing like a jinx to get her stomach all twisted. "We need a plan B, just in case."

"We don't have time for plan B. We only have plan A, and trust me…it'll work." He kissed her softly. "I want you in my life, Lexi."

Her stomach got that weird fluttery feeling that comes with all the good things. "You do?"

He was looking at her again, his eyes penetrating and very, very sincere. "I know what it's like to live in darkness, Lexi. My family is fucked, and growing up with that life messed me up. I've never felt the way I feel now—like there's hope, like I can be happy. All my life, I was told that I would run my family one day, that I would take over for my father. He wants me to be a

146

person I can't be. That's why I ran. That's why I became Sam Henderson. He can never find out who I really am, because I don't want him to destroy who I've become. You understand that because you're running too."

Am I running? She hadn't thought of it like that.

He shook his head. "I'm going to get this story, and you're going to protect Sabine, then we're going to be together, like we're meant to be. Give Devon what he wants and meet me at the airport. It'll all work out. You'll see."

Lexi believed him. Okay, she *wanted* to believe him. *Shit!* "Fine."

The plans still felt shaky where Sabine was concerned, but at least Devon wouldn't get anywhere close to the database, and if Sam succeeded, the Highwaymen and the Riders would be arrested before they could do any damage.

"I'll have to call Sabine and let her know what's going on."

"Yes, once it's over, for sure, but until then, this is between us."

"But—"

"You promised not to share my identity with her."

"I won't even mention your actual name."

"I can't take that risk…not right now. Please, Lexi, just wait until this is all said and done, once we're back in New York."

Lexi gulped down the lump in her throat.

"I've got an FBI contact. I called him and filled him in on the details. He'll arrest the Highwaymen and the Riders as soon as I can get him the evidence, and he'll let me run with the story idea I have planned."

Okay, the FBI being involved made her feel a little better.

Sam pulled her into his chest, holding her in a bear hug that made her feel cherished and comforted. Sam was a strong man, a smart man—and he was a very skilled investigator. She should trust him on this and let him take the lead like she'd agreed to.

"Okay, I'm still in. Show me this database you've created."

Chapter Fifteen

Lexi was grateful that Sam wasn't pushing her about the real database, because, of course, there was one. Lexi would never confirm that fact to anyone, not even Sam, but she was glad he hadn't demanded to know. It proved to her that he wasn't just saying pretty words when he'd told her he wanted her in his life. He respected her boundaries enough to let them be—and that was big deal to Lexi.

Lexi clicked open another sub-file in the fake database that Sam had created for Devon. The information he'd put into his false database was amusing. She'd laughed out loud a few times at the presumably made-up details Sam had created about a lot of prominent people, which gave her an idea of what he truly thought about some of the senators, politicians, celebrities and other important social figures. He wasn't one of those people who was enamored by wealth and power, that was for sure. What was most interesting to Lexi, though, was that some of the information Sam had 'made up' was actually hitting pretty close to the truth. Whether he'd known more than he let on or had made some educated guesses, Lexi didn't know, but he'd written 'on the mark' details about some of the men he'd listed in his database. He'd even created a file on Devon and filled it with what Lexi could only assume was accurate information based on his own firsthand knowledge of the man. It sounded believable from what she knew of the socialite, and it was scandalous enough to make Devon believe it was the real deal.

The database itself didn't look anything like the one the Kitty Cats used, but Devon wouldn't know that. Overall, she was impressed with what Sam had put together in such a short amount of time, and she was feeling a lot more confident that it would appease and distract Devon enough so that she could get off the yacht and to the airport without him suspecting anything. The plan seemed pretty solid... Well, except for Sam's part in it.

She sighed and closed the file she'd been reading on Devon. Sam was in the shower, soaping up because he hadn't had a chance to when he'd been in there with her earlier. A smile crept over her lips when she thought about how he'd cared for her. He wanted her in his life, and there was no denying she wanted the same thing. Even though she was broken and couldn't be what she'd used to be, he understood and accepted that, probably because he had demons too. She wanted to see how this played out between them. Would the chemistry last? She felt like it would. She had never experienced something so powerful with another person, and she really didn't want to be apart from him, so that was something, right?

Even though she wanted to join him in the shower, give back a little of what he'd given her, time was running out and he had an appointment to keep. It was the meeting that really didn't sit well with her. Despite his assurances, it was too dangerous. The men he was messing with hadn't become successful thieves because they were good guys. She was sure that with a little digging she'd find a lot of skeletons in their closets…figuratively and literally, which was probably why this was such a huge draw for Sam.

Even though Sam came from a crime family himself, she had her doubts that he could really anticipate everything that could possibly go wrong at this meeting. Was he putting too much faith in his abilities as an investigative reporter? She wasn't sure. She hoped not. Her stomach wasn't convinced, though, and she was dealing with knots that made her sick with worry.

She scanned Sam's laptop. He had to have at least a hundred files on his desktop alone. She assumed they were partial stories or investigations he was working on. There was nothing for her to be snooping through, even though she was sorely tempted to…old habits from her Kitty Cat days. Any information was good information as far as Sabine was concerned. Lexi put her hand on the top of the lid and was starting to close the laptop when her gaze landed on a file she *had* to open.

NGL.

National Gymnastics League. It had to be. She'd seen him on the website earlier but hadn't pursued it because she'd gotten distracted by his urgency to tell her his plan. Why had he been on the NGL website and why did he have a file with that exact acronym? She moved the mouse to hover over the file then hesitated for a second. Did she really want to know?

Yes.

She clicked it open and started to read.

Sam stepped out of the bathroom fully dressed and ready to rendezvous with Dax and Vince. He felt confident... Okay, he felt *mostly* confident that things would go the way he'd planned.

Until he saw Lexi seated at the desk, leaning into his computer like she was riveted to something, something he probably should have done a better job hiding. No...something he maybe should have told her about and not let her find on her own like this, without an explanation.

"I can explain. I was going to tell — "

She snapped her eyes to meet his and the look of betrayal there was like a shot to his heart. "You wrote down everything I told you. Every word I said is here." She let out a bitter laugh. "Did you record me or something?"

"No, of course not." He frowned. "I wasn't planning on running with it until I'd spoken to you."

"Spoken to me because you wanted consent or because you wanted to inform me that you were going to put it out there?" She crossed her arms and leaned back in the chair, giving Sam a narrow-eyed look that let him know there was only one right answer.

"I'm a reporter, Lexi. I reveal injustices. I fight for the vulnerable. I make sure the stories that need to be heard are heard. This story needs to be heard." He pointed to his computer. "I started writing that way before I even knew the details of your injury."

She nodded. "Yes, I can see that." She leaned forward and scrolled through the document she was on. "You started writing it the day after my injury, actually. Is that why you've been so invested in me? Because you finally want to wrap up this little story of yours? Was that your plan, to get me to lower my defenses so I would tell you—"

"Fuck no!" he growled. "Of course not, Lexi! That wasn't my plan at all. I've been upfront with you about what I'm doing here. I haven't lied to you about any of it. I haven't kept things from you either." He didn't say, *like you have*, but he wanted to. She was the one keeping the database's existence a secret from him, like she didn't trust him with even that little bit of information.

"Well, now I'm doubly glad that I didn't give you any more information about anything. I thought I was talking to Sam, my friend, my lover, my—" She seemed to choke on her next words.

"Lexi, come on."

"But I was talking to Sam Henderson, the reporter. What's your slogan? *'If there's a story, I'll find it.'*"

"I wasn't going to sell the story, not unless you were okay with it. I'd planned on sharing the proceeds with you. Whatever I made, you'd get seventy percent." He took a step in her direction, but the look she gave him cut him to the core. That definitely had been the wrong thing to say.

"This isn't about money." She pushed the chair back and got up. Her body was tense, like a coiled snake ready to strike. "I trusted you with that information."

"I know, and I wasn't going to betray your trust, I swear—but, Lexi, this story is important. Think of all the other ways the league is silencing women and girls. Can you not see how this could be used to cover up so many horrible things? Maybe things that didn't happen to you but things that have happened or are currently happening to other girls?"

"What are you talking about?" She crossed her arms.

He pointed to the laptop. "If you read through the documents, you'll see the allegations of sexual assault and misconduct that have been covered up for years, decades."

"Seems unsubstantiated."

Sam's mouth dropped open. He couldn't believe the depth of Lexi's denial. "Are you serious?"

"Sam, you can't throw accusations around just because of rumors. The dreams of thousands of gymnasts are tied up in this organization. You could jeopardize all that with a story that has no proof."

"The proof would come if we blew the whistle on what happened to you. There would be an active investigation by the FBI."

"Let me guess... Your FBI pal has told you so?" She snorted. "And what? They'll dismantle the organization so that there is no competition this year? Or maybe never again? Athletes are competing to qualify for the Olympics in eight weeks. Do you think your story will blow over by then? I don't. I think you'll open a can of worms in the name of saving a lot of victims only to create more. You don't understand how this works!"

"So, help me understand, Lexi! Work with me so we can make this safe for everyone but still bring the evil shit that's going on to light." He moved closer to her. "What your coach did to you was despicable. The world should know about it. You said he left the country. Have you looked him up?"

"No, of course not. I never want to see Claude again."

Sam moved to his laptop and typed a web address in. "Look at what he's up to." He turned the screen so she could see. Claude's profile picture and details were listed. He was coaching the Russian team.

She scanned the site, her eyes growing wide. "He's not allowed…"

"He's a renowned coach with no blemishes on his records because the NGL covered it up and gave him a free pass."

Lexi covered her mouth and tears bubbled to her eyes. "He'll do it to someone else."

"Yes, he likely will."

Lexi's whole body seemed to cave in on itself. She deflated right before his eyes. Sam moved to her, taking her in his arms, and she didn't resist. "We can figure this out, Lexi. Once this is all over with Devon, we'll work on the story together and make it so that no one else gets hurt." He kissed the top of her head.

She wrapped her arms around him and nodded. "Don't go to this meeting."

"I have to." He kissed her again then pulled back, untangling himself from her. "Everything will work out. I promise."

"Sam—"

"I'm not giving up this story. I'm too close." He moved to the other side of the room, turning his back on her expression, because if he looked at her for a second longer, he'd lose his resolve to see it through.

"There are some things that are not worth the risk." Her tone let him know that she was finally understanding how much he'd do and how far he'd go to get a story.

"This is." He put his phone in his pocket. "I'm meeting a contact from the field in twenty minutes so he can wire me up. I'll call you the second I leave the meeting."

"Sam, I have a bad feeling."

"Have some faith. I'm good at what I do." He walked to the door, pausing only long enough give Lexi a look that he hoped conveyed confidence, even though he knew her words were going to haunt him until the meeting was over.

Chapter Sixteen

Lexi's bad feeling kept getting worse as the minutes ticked by. She was dressed, her hair and makeup done, waiting on Devon for their meeting, but he was nowhere to be found. The yacht staff didn't even know where he was.

As they'd planned, she had packed her bag and gathered up everything, including Sam's laptop and duffel bag. If she was going to make a run for it, she needed to be ready.

Now she waited.

She contemplated calling Sabine, but when Lexi thought about what she'd say to her ex-boss, she kind of stalled out. What could she tell Sabine that would do any good? That she was avoiding a security breach by using a fake database? That Sam had gone to a meeting with some really sketchy criminals?

No, there was nothing to report. No imminent threat. *And yet...* And yet, Lexi couldn't stop worrying that they had mis-stepped somehow. Even though Sam had assured her that he'd done this before and she believed that he was good at investigating and getting his story, she still had misgivings about it all.

Bang, bang, bang. Lexi stifled a yelp and turned toward the door. "Lexi, baby, you in there?" Devon turned the knob.

"I'm coming!" Lexi didn't want him to see the packed bags, so she rushed to intercept him before he could get a peek inside. She shoved herself into his body, bullying him back as she moved out of the cabin. "It's hot in there. Steamed up the whole cabin with my shower." She giggled because she knew Devon was the sort of man who liked a giggler.

He looked her up and down, his eyes telling her everything she needed to know. Friendship or not, he'd betray Sam if given the chance. Lexi gave him a look back that should make her message clear. *Not a chance.*

He winked at her, obviously not easily dissuaded. He curled his lips into a predatory smile then slipped his arm around her waist. "Let's get our deal underway, shall we?" He led her down the hallway toward his suite. "Sam's on his way to a meeting himself, isn't he?"

Lexi frowned. Would Devon know all about that? Was he testing her? Or was he fishing? "He left about an hour ago." And why did she feel so vulnerable all of a sudden? Was it the way Devon was leering at her? Or maybe how he was tightening his hold on her waist like he was scared she was going to take off?

"So, we're all alone." Devon smirked. "Whatever will we do once our deal is sorted?"

"I'm sure we'll figure something out." Lexi let her voice dip into her Kitty Cat sensual tone. It was the easiest way to get men to do what she wanted. Even though Devon's hands on her now were making her feel gross, she pushed on. She had a job to do.

Devon ran his hand over her hip. "Yes, I'm sure we will."

He opened the door to his suite and motioned for her to enter. "I'm going to need a bank number from you — somewhere to send the agreed-upon sum."

Lexi frowned. Right. She had a bank account, but fuck if she knew the account number. Devon, catching her expression of confusion, said, "Or, I could set up something with the bank I use."

He'd likely figure out some way to withhold the money, not that she had really expected him to pay up in the first place. She smiled, giving an expression of relief. "Sure, yes, that sounds like a great idea." She didn't need his money, and since the database wasn't even real anyway, she didn't have to worry about swindling him either.

"Perfect." Devon guided her toward the desk where his laptop was already open and waiting. "I'll make a call and get that sorted out for you. Here... Take a seat and get started on your end of the deal."

Lexi gulped and hoped her smile hid her nervousness. What if the database wasn't real enough to fool Devon? What would he do if he realized she was lying to him?

She sat down at the desk and put her hands on the keyboard, willing her fingers not to shake.

Devon nodded then put his phone to his ear and walked away. "Hey, Murray, yeah, I need you to set up an account for a bank transfer. Account holder name is Lexi Monroe."

Lexi tuned Devon out and typed in the address of the site Sam had created. She held her breath, half expecting it not to load now that she was on Devon's computer. Much to her relief, it did, looking just like it had when she'd checked it earlier. She logged in and the program opened to show the files all laid out.

Devon came up behind her and whistled. "That sneaky woman has a lot of information, doesn't she? I bet she has all you girls collecting for her, right?" He didn't wait for an answer, just waved Lexi to move, which she did, then he took her seat. He leaned in to the screen, scanning the files quickly. "How many are in here?"

"Too many to count." Lexi felt like she was walking a tightrope of lies. If Devon started to click too deeply, he'd figure out really quickly how shallow the actual files were. Sam had taken a gamble on what information would draw Devon's attention.

"Senator Russell is in here?" He laughed. "You've got to be kidding me!" He clicked open that file first, and thankfully it was full of documents. "We went to school with his kid, Stephen. What a fuck-up that guy was."

Lexi wanted to slip out now, get her and Sam's stuff and hail a cab, but she was rooted in place, watching Devon explore the files. He moved the cursor, clicking through the various subfolders.

"Where's mine?"

Lexi leaned over him and navigated to Devon's folder. "Right here." She cleared her throat. "This information is highly confidential. You probably should keep that in mind before you do anything—"

"Lexi, baby, you have nothing to worry about. You're a millionaire." He picked up his phone. "Give me your email and I'll send you the link to your off-shore account."

She did as he asked, and within seconds, her phone binged with an incoming email.

"Go ahead. See for yourself." She opened her phone and clicked on the email. It looked legit, complete with account information and the total amount transferred. "All you'll have to do is call the bank and claim the funds. You can have them transferred to any bank in America, although I would recommend keeping the money in this account. Tax haven." He turned back to the computer.

Lexi didn't believe for one second that the money was actually hers to take, but as far as Devon was concerned, the deal was done.

"Son of a bitch! How did she know that happened to me?" Devon was riveted to the screen. He was so engrossed that Lexi made it all the way to the door before he noticed she was trying to leave. "Where do you think you're going? We have plans." Devon made a valiant effort to tear himself away from the computer screen.

"Oh, I thought I'd give you some time to read the file and go put on something a little more comfortable." She ran her hands along her form-fitting dress. "Maybe something a little less restrictive."

A hungry-looking smile spread on Devon's face and he gave her one of his off-putting once-overs. "Sounds like a good plan, baby. Be quick. I'm a fast reader."

Lexi's heart was already racing, but hearing those words put her into overdrive. "I won't be long," she said as she closed the door behind her then speed walked back to her cabin.

She grabbed the two bags and exited quickly, making it to the deck in a matter of seconds.

"Oh, Ms. Monroe, is there something I can do for you?" Rose, the cleaning lady Lexi had spoken to earlier, was wiping down a handrail. She looked at Lexi's arms, laden with two bags, her eyes going wide. "Are you leaving?"

"Yes, I am. There's a family emergency. I need a cab."

Rose snapped her fingers at a guy who was standing by the dock. "Jim, can you notify Mr. Caldone's driver that Miss Monroe needs a ride?"

Lexi winced. She didn't want to take Devon's car, because then he'd know where she was going, but she didn't see any taxis idling anywhere either — and she needed to be gone now. "Thank you, Rose!" Like Sam said, sometimes a person needed to take some risks to get some action.

Jim nodded. "Follow me, Miss." He handled her bags as she started down the ramp.

It took her less than two minutes to get into the limo and another minute more to be on the road and headed to the airport, but she didn't breathe a sigh of relief until they were on the highway and she could see the planes coming in and taking off.

Even if Devon figured out what was going on, that she had left, he wouldn't go to too much trouble to track her down. She hoped anyway. He had what he wanted...or thought he did.

She kept looking at her phone, praying for a text or a call from Sam, letting her know that he was on his way too, but it was silent. It was likely too early to be hearing from him.

She thanked the driver once they reached the airport and took her bags inside herself. Sam had said he'd chartered a private plane for them, but she had no idea where to even begin looking for that terminal.

Fuck.

She looked at her phone. Should she try calling Sam? Would she be putting him at risk if she did? She was antsy, wanting to get onto a plane and the hell away from Key West.

Her phone rang, startling her enough that she jumped. "Hello?"

"Lexi, it's Sam. Listen… Are you at the airport yet?"

"Sam, what phone are you calling from?" His number was coming up as 'unknown'. "Where are you?"

"Lexi, are you at the airport?" His voice was like a whip.

"Yes. I just got here but I don't know where to go."

"Okay, you need to get out of there right now."

"Excuse me, Miss. But are you Lexi Monroe?" Two security guards flanked her.

"I am."

"Lexi!" Sam was shouting, his voice clear even to the security guards. "You have to get out of there right now. Don't go with them. Don't—"

The call disconnected. A wash of fear ran through Lexi and spiked her anxiety. She glanced quickly at the nearest exit.

One of the security guards grabbed her elbow tightly. "You're going to have to come with us."

"What? No, I don't have to go anywhere with you. I demand to know what this is about."

The other security guard took her other arm, wrenching it behind her back painfully. "Be quiet and don't make a scene"—he leaned closer—"or your boyfriend won't make it home tonight." He plucked her phone from her hand then slipped it into his pocket.

Lexi stopped struggling, if only to keep her arm from being snapped in half. "I want to make a call. I get one phone call, right?"

"You're not under arrest." The guard holding her elbow was all but dragging her past the security gate to a pair of double doors.

"If I'm not under arrest, then let me go!" She made sure her voice was loud enough for the travelers around her to see. She caught the eye of a woman who was watching and knew her best strategy would be a tried and tested one. She started crying. "I don't understand what's going on!" More people stopped to look. The guard holding her arms tightened his grip. "Please, let me make a call. I have to let my boss know that I'm going to be late or else I'll be fired. Please... I don't know what I did wrong, but if you'd let me —"

"Oh, for fuck's sake." The guard walking ahead of her stopped abruptly. He lifted his hand to rub at his face, like he really didn't need this shit today. "Give her the phone back."

The guard holding her arm released his grip slightly. "Make your call then."

She stumbled a step, but the guard holding her elbow kept her from falling on her face.

"Thank you! I'll be quick. I promise."

He leaned in so he could speak quietly. "If you do anything foolish, you'll regret it, Lexi," he growled, then dug her phone out of his pocket and handed it to her.

She quickly typed in the passcode then hit the contact she needed. It rang three times. Three excruciating rings, and all the while Lexi prayed that she hadn't made the wrong decision, that the emergency number would still work for her.

"Lexi, what's wrong?"

She let out the breath she was holding. "Adam, hi, bad news. I'm going to be late for my next appointment."

Chapter Seventeen

Sam wasn't quite sure where things had gone wrong. He didn't know if he'd walked into a trap or if he'd said something to trigger one, but either way he was nursing a headache that felt like a thousand baseball bats were pounding his skull, and he was fairly confident that he was riding in the trunk of a car. He couldn't see anything because of the burlap-like bag over his head, but he could smell a faint scent of gasoline. His arms were tied behind his back. He'd awoken completely discombobulated and in pain, with no memory of how he'd actually gotten where he was. Strangely, he wasn't scared, though. Maybe that was because of his head injury — or maybe it was because he was damn stupid.

If he was in a car, it wasn't moving. He couldn't hear shit either, so he had no clues as to where they'd taken him or how long he'd been unconscious for.

The last thing he remembered was leaving Lexi to meet his buddy who was going to wire him up for his meeting with the Highwaymen and the Riders. He had no idea what had happened after that. Had he made it to the meeting? Had he even gotten in the front door? He hoped like hell that Lexi had made it off the yacht and to the airport. Their chartered flight would take off at four a.m. That was what he'd told the pilot Teddy, another buddy of his, to do, regardless of if he made it or not. Teddy would be on the lookout for Lexi at the airport and would make sure she boarded safely. Getting her out of there was his only concern, even though he'd told Lexi that the plane wouldn't leave until they were both on board. His head hurt too much to think hard about it all, though. He wished he could remember what the last few hours had involved.

Sam tried to move, to test the limits of his confinement, but every twitch of his muscles sent shooting pain through his entire body. Was that what Lexi felt on a daily basis? Sam would kill for a few of her pain meds right about now. He breathed through the pain and let his body relax as much as possible, which wasn't a lot, considering he was crammed into someone's trunk and could end up dead at any moment.

"Get him out."

Sam heard the muffled command seconds before the trunk popped open. The bag over his head was removed swiftly, taking some of his hair with it. He wasn't blinded by light, but his eyes hurt all the same. Wherever they were, it was still dark out. He didn't recognize the guys wrenching him out of the trunk either, but that wasn't saying much, considering the size of Dax's and Vince's gangs.

"You cause any trouble, Mr. Henderson, and I'll wallop you again," the bigger of the two men said, his voice eerily calm. Sam looked at the dude's meaty hands and realized that if he'd been the one to hit Sam the first time, well, it was no wonder he couldn't remember shit.

Mr. Henderson. The realization dawned slowly that the guy had called him by his alias. *Ohhhhh, shit.* Jolts of memory filtered into his scattered brain. He'd made it to the meeting, but things had been all wrong right from the start. He'd called Lexi...

Sam's stomach pitched. Lexi was in trouble.

The guys dragged him out, not caring in the least that he couldn't balance himself at all. When he pitched forward, almost smashing his face into the ground, he realized where they were — back at the boat. His suspicions were confirmed a minute later as they dragged Sam between them up the walkway and onto Devon's yacht.

He tried to get his feet under him, but he couldn't coordinate himself. The guys dragging him kept moving, ignoring Sam's efforts to gain control. Where was Lexi? What had happened to her? He didn't dare ask for fear that he'd find out the worst.

"Samuel...or should I just call you Sam?" Dax was seated on the leather wrap-around couch with his feet up and his arms behind his head, looking relaxed and completely unfazed.

Devon was seated at the other end, his head lolling forward, blood dripping slowly from a wound Sam couldn't see. He was propped up by the armrest, his hands tied behind his back.

"What happened?" Sam was genuinely confused. Obviously, his plan had backfired somehow, but how had Devon gone from partner to victim in this situation?

"What happened?" Dax laughed as he planted his feet on the wood floor and sat upright, steepling his hands in front of him. "Well, let's see… You forgot who you were dealing with, Sam Henderson, award-winning investigative reporter." His voice rose slightly. "You forgot that I have access to more information than you can imagine and that I've seen it all. I'll give you props for the database—that was clever—but even a fool like Devon figured out it was a fake. Maybe not as quickly as I would have, but he proved his loyalty in the end."

"What did you do to him? If he's so loyal, why does he look like he's been pummeled?"

"Because he let your girl slip away." Vince stepped into the room with two guys behind him, who were carrying something. "And I've got a temper."

"Let me go!" Lexi's muffled yell sent a chill straight to Sam's gut. Her head was covered, just as his had been, and she was struggling in her captor's arms.

The guys dumped her to the ground, and she landed with a thud. She was quiet for a few seconds, likely collecting herself, because Sam knew that fall had to have jarred her back and sent screaming pain through her entire body. It didn't keep her down, though. No, she pushed herself up to her knees and started yelling again.

"Take this thing off my head! I can't breathe in here."

Dax nodded at one of the guys, who moved forward and whipped the bag off her head.

Her hair flew up then landed in a mess on her face. Her arms were tied behind her back so she couldn't clear her vision. The guy who'd ripped the bag off moved forward and brushed her hair from her face. Seeing that thug's fingers on Lexi had Sam's hackles rising. He wanted to tell him to get his hands off her, but Lexi handled it with much more grace…and balls.

"I would appreciate you not touching me. You have to pay for that privilege."

Dax barked a laugh, his face showing what looked like appreciation for her gall.

Sam admired her courage. Here she was, taking in the scene before her — Devon's bloody face, Sam tied up, and yet she returned her gaze to Dax's and met him head-on.

"Why have you kidnapped me?"

Dax snorted another laugh. "You have access to something I want."

She shifted a look toward Sam and he saw, for a split second, fear flash in her eyes.

"I was just saying to your friend, Sam, that your fake database bought you some time, but sadly, not enough. Good effort, though." Dax stood and crossed the room. "Now you're going to access Sabine's real database right here, right now."

"I won't." Lexi straightened her back and glared at Dax.

Vince moved forward in a flash then smacked the back of her head hard enough to send her flying forward. With no hands to brace her fall, she landed hard, the side of her face taking the brunt of it.

"Don't fucking touch her!" Sam roared. Fuck, he wanted to kill these assholes with his bare hands.

"You be quiet, you lying sack of shit." Dax brought a laptop over to the coffee table. "Help her up."

Lexi's nose was bleeding and her cheek was red. One of Vince's men hauled her to her knees. Somehow, Lexi stifled the yelp of pain Sam could see clearly on her face.

Dax crowded her, so close that Sam could see spit hitting her cheek as he spoke. "You'll access the database right fucking now."

"And if I don't?"

Dax flicked his eyes to one of Vince's guys, who in turn pulled a gun from the back of his pants then shot Devon in the head. No hesitation.

Lexi screamed. Sam's entire understanding of the situation shift as he watched his friend's brains slide down the cushion of the couch.

"Get rid of him," Vince ordered.

Lexi was whimpering quietly as the men removed Devon's body. She turned her head and mouthed, *I'm sorry*, to Sam.

He shook his head. *Not your fault.*

"If you don't access the database within the next twenty seconds, I'll shoot your boyfriend in the head too. So, what'd you say, Lexi? Ready to cooperate?"

Lexi sniffled, then snapped her gaze to Dax. "Yes."

"Untie her." Dax moved the computer closer to Lexi before turning his attention to Sam. "And you. What will I do with you, Sam Henderson?"

Lexi snapped her head up. "You can call his father and demand a meeting."

"His father?" Dax snorted. "Mr. Henderson? This guy has been lying to you too, princess."

Lexi opened her mouth, but Dax cut her off before she could speak.

"He was impersonating Samuel Dove, and I've got to say, the resemblance is close. Really close. No way would Fredrick Dove allow his son to become a soul-sucking reporter, not with the number of bodies he has buried in his backyard."

"Allegedly," Sam said.

Dax laughed. "Right. The man is so smooth that nothing has ever been proven. A fucking reporter like you would know that, right? The Dove family must be the holy fucking grail to a lowlife like you." Dax shook his head. "I should have known that Devon would fuck this up. when he was bragging about knowing Samuel Dove, about getting us a connection to his father. Devon was full of shit and stupid as fuck, but he had more money than he knew what to do with, sooo...yeah." Dax shrugged as if it was no big deal that he'd murdered a guy over being stupid and trusting. "You probably shouldn't have worn a wire to our meeting." Dax put his hand out and one of his men gave him a gun. He checked that it was loaded. "That was a stupid move for such a seasoned reporter." He pulled the slide back and chambered a round. "At first I thought DEA, maybe FBI, but no, you're just a lying piece of shit reporter who stuck his nose in the wrong place." He pointed the gun at Sam's head. "Access the fucking database now, Lexi!"

Lexi flinched, but she put her hands on the laptop. She typed quickly. "Here, here. I did it. You're in."

Dax smiled. "Turn the computer toward me."

Lexi did as she was told.

"Good girl." He lowered the gun then sat down on the couch. "See? Everything works out when you cooperate." He put the gun on the table then pulled the laptop toward him and started typing, a slow smile creeping on his face. "It would have made things way easier to have access to Fredrick Dove for our plan, but without a proper introduction, well, we'll have to use plan B."

"You want to destroy Sabine?" Lexi asked, her voice a little shaky. One of the men behind her raised his hand as if to strike her, but Dax motioned for him to stop without taking his eyes off the screen.

"No, I'll answer that." Dax's smile grew. "Yes, I plan to destroy Sabine Cowan. I plan to steal her money. I plan to create enemies for her by selling all this information she's gathered. She'll be dead before the end of the week if I play this right—and my hands will be clean."

"Then what?" Sam asked. "You fund another charity with the proceeds? Buy yourself an island? Traffic some women there?" Because as much as Dax wanted people to believe that he was all Robin Hood with the money he stole, Sam had uncovered quite a few dark and disgusting uses of the funds he'd taken over the years.

Dax snapped his eyes up to Sam's. "See? This is why I fucking hate reporters. You assholes never know when to shut up." He raised the gun again, pointing it at Sam. "I will use the money to grease some of the people I associate with. Keeping my people happy ensures my success and, as you know, I'm not leading the biggest gang in existence, so I must do what I must do." He shrugged. "But after you're dead, the threat of anyone finding that out will be gone."

He stood up and put the gun to Sam's head, pushing hard into his temple. Sam kept his eyes on Lexi. They weren't getting out of this alive, and he wanted her to know how fucking sorry he was for that.

"Say goodbye to Sam, Lexi."

"She has nothing to do with this," Sam growled. "She's good at keeping secrets."

Dax nodded. "So?"

"So, kill me but let her go."

Dax snorted. "I don't think so. She knows too much at this point. You know that." He jammed the gun harder against Sam's head. "I admire your balls though, Sam. For a reporter, you're probably a stand-up guy." He pulled the gun back then leaned forward so he was right in Sam's face. "I'll make sure it's painless for her, okay? Mostly painless, anyway." Then he winked.

Sam roared. He reeled back and rammed his head against Dax's, sending the man stumbling backward.

A gun went off, so loud that Sam was deafened by the noise. He fell to the side, landing hard on his shoulder. *Am I dead? Dying?* He couldn't tell.

More guns went off. There was screaming. Moaning. People were running—or trying to.

Sam tried to see Lexi in all the commotion, but she wasn't where he'd last seen her. He pushed himself up, only to feel the muzzle of a gun press to his temple once again.

"You're coming with me." Dax was bleeding from somewhere, his shirt soaking through with the red stuff, but all the same, he hauled Sam up, using him as a shield as they moved through the carnage to the door.

Sam couldn't see Lexi anywhere. She wasn't on the floor. She wasn't bleeding out. He fucking hoped she'd managed to escape somehow.

"I don't know what the fuck is going on here, but—"

"You'll kindly take your hands off my son." Fredrick Dove loomed in the doorway, a gun in his hand, flanked by more of his men.

"Y-y-your son?" Dax was shaking. "But...he's... a..."

"Reporter, yes. Disappointing, I know, but you've got to let them sow their oats however they see fit." Sam's father motioned to Dax with his gun. "Release him now."

"I'm sorry, sir." Dax let Sam go and took a step away. "It was a misunderstanding. If I had known—" Another shot rang out and Dax's words stopped. His body hit the floor seconds after that.

"Father," Sam said, wondering how in the world his father had found him.

"Son." Sam's father moved into the room. "We have your girl safely in the hands of her people."

"Her people?" Sam turned so that his father could untie him.

"Adam Lancaster reached out and filled me in on what was going down. We coordinated a rescue."

Adam Lancaster? Sabine's head of security? How? Then he realized... Lexi had betrayed his secret to Adam. She'd broken her promise to Sam and had told Adam who he really was, who his father was. He didn't know how she'd done it, but she had. Despite how irrational it was for him to be angry given the circumstances, he was.

"I know you value your privacy, but she saved your life, son." His father patted him on the back and Sam was mortified that his father could read him that easily. "Let's go get you checked out. Your eyes look a little glassy."

"What about all this?" Sam took in the carnage, the blood, the brains, the dead bodies.

"Adam's team will take care of this mess." Sam's father took his arm, not in a forceful way, but Sam knew he really didn't have a choice. "Come with me, son. We'll get you sorted out. It's time to come home."

And just like that, Sam knew he'd been sucked right back into his father's world—and he had Lexi to thank for it.

Chapter Eighteen

Weeks later

Lexi was still having nightmares, but for a change, they weren't about her gymnastics accident. She kept alternating between watching Devon's brains splatter against the leather couch and the chaos of the gunfight that had happened shortly after that. She could still feel the burning sensation of a bullet skidding past her cheek, a fraction of an inch away from obliterating her life. It had completely healed and hadn't left a scar, but still, even in the dark, Lexi could trace the path it had taken. Those dreams were worse than her accident dreams. She woke up screaming and crying, dread flooding all her senses as she remembered the horrific scene that had been her reality all those weeks ago.

She knew that if Sam were with her, she wouldn't have any nightmares—or at least, she'd have someone there to comfort her if she did. For the two nights she'd spent with him, she'd slept blissfully after he'd satiated her darkest needs, and she could only fantasize over how he'd take care of her in the aftermath of what they'd experienced together. But she couldn't have him, now or ever. She'd betrayed his trust and had broken a promise to keep his identity a secret from Sabine, and now Sam Henderson-Dove had his very own file in the Cowan database, she was sure. Sabine wasn't one to waste valuable information.

When Lexi had been detained at the airport and granted one call, she had known that whatever she said to Adam had to mean something so that she would put him on the right track. The fact that she'd called the emergency number had been enough to alert him that something was wrong, but when she'd told him that she was going to miss an appointment with Samuel Dove, she'd hoped like hell he'd picked up on the clue and figured out who she meant.

Of course, Adam being Adam, he had. He'd also tracked her down right at the very moment that all hell had broken loose on the yacht. She'd known Adam was good, but she hadn't realized how good he was until his right-hand man Brett had wrapped his strong arms around her while she'd trembled on the floor, certain she was about to get hit by another bullet. Brett had pulled her out of that situation like it was the most natural thing in the world and had taken her to a Cowan medic within minutes. Adam had shown up a few hours later and she'd been whisked away on Sabine's private jet shortly after that. Of course, both Brett and Adam had assured her that Sam was alive and unhurt and that his father had coordinated with Adam's team to deal with the situation. She knew what that meant for Sam. Now that his father was back in his life, he'd never let Sam go.

She'd known that would happen when she'd told Adam who Sam really was, but she'd felt the sacrifice would be worth it if she saved his life—and by extension her own. She knew what she'd done would effectively end any warm feelings Sam might have for her, and while that made her extremely sad, she wouldn't have done anything differently.

All the same, after three weeks of thinking hard on it, she'd finally settled on how to try to make it up to him. It was maybe a no-brainer, but it had taken her some time to accept the truth of what he'd said to her on the yacht all those weeks before. She needed to speak up about what had happened to her and how the NGL had silenced her, like they'd silenced many athletes before her.

It had taken her some time, but she'd compiled a document of her experience and had even contacted some of the gymnasts she used to train with to get statements from them as well. She'd given Sam a list of names that he could reach out to, people who would speak to him only because she'd asked them to.

She'd sent the email hours ago and wasn't expecting a reply, so when her phone rang with Sam's number flashing on the screen, she was so taken aback that she almost missed his call.

"Hello?"

"Lexi." His voice was full of emotion, a gruffness that told her so much about how she'd hurt him. "I got your email."

She gulped down the lump in her throat. "I thought maybe it would help."

"I passed it along to one of my colleagues."

"Oh." Her heart sank with his rejection of her peace offering. "I thought maybe you'd want to run with it."

Why didn't he want it now? Was he so angry with her that he was willing to sabotage his own future, give up a story that would give him what he had so badly wanted only a few weeks before? She knew how much getting the story meant to him.

"Can't." He took a deep breath. "Sam Henderson has retired."

Her stomach pitched. "Because of your father?" She hadn't meant to destroy his alias.

"Partly." He cleared his throat. "But also because I've accepted a new position."

"Oh?" She wasn't going to pry. She'd already messed things up for him in huge ways, but she was hoping he'd tell her. He didn't owe her peace of mind, though. "I'm sorry, Sam. I thought what I was doing was the only way. I was scared."

"It's okay, Lexi." Sam sighed. "Eventually my father would have forced his way back into my life. It was only a matter of time. He already knew about my alias." Sam let out a bitter-sounding laugh.

"Yes, but now you owe him something, right? Because he saved you?"

"I've always owed him something." He grunted another laugh. "Things are complicated." And he'd been trying to avoid complicating his life with his father's shit. She knew that.

"Again, I'm sorry, Sam."

"You did what you had to do." He didn't sound convinced.

All the same, his words eased her mind a bit. "But you're disappointed that I betrayed your trust, right?"

"I betrayed your trust too. I should never have written down your story about your accident without your consent."

"But you were right about that. I needed to share my story. I see that now."

"And you were right to out my real identity to Sabine. I see *that* now." His tone was flat, contrary to his words.

She gasped. She'd never in a million years thought that he'd say that. "Even though I ruined your career?"

"Well, you also opened a door for me, one that maybe wasn't there before."

Lexi frowned. "I did?"

"Yes, but we can talk about it when I see you."

Lexi was stunned speechless. Her mouth was hanging open and she was glad Sam couldn't see her.

"Lexi? You there?"

"Uh…yeah…I am."

"There's a car waiting downstairs for you. It'll bring you to me."

Her heart ramped up and her body coiled. "Okay."

"I'll see you soon." Then he hung up and Lexi stared at her phone like she could make sense of the way things had turned out.

He wants to see me! He wasn't so angry that he would hate her forever. That was something, right? Lexi scrambled to collect her things. She grabbed her purse, checking to make sure her pain meds were inside, then shoved her phone in there too. She checked her reflection, thankful that she'd done a deep conditioning treatment on her hair that morning. It was so silky and bouncy that Sam would love running his fingers through it. She checked herself with that thought. He'd said they would talk, nothing more than that. Better that she didn't get carried away with ideas of him wanting her still. Maybe he wanted to talk in person so he could stress his boundaries to her now that he was back with his family. He hadn't sounded like himself. She couldn't detect even a little bit of happiness in his voice. Had she ruined things so much that he couldn't even be himself?

She deflated a bit. *Right.* Better to keep things realistic. His tone hadn't given her any reason to think he was excited to see her. This was probably business for him now. Taking care of loose ends, not that she thought he was capable of hurting her, not even if his father was making him take over the family business. No, what she was dreading was a lecture about all the ways she'd messed up his life. That was what she deserved. She locked her condo door and made her way down to the lobby.

"Ms. Monroe, there's a limo waiting for you," George, the doorman, said as he rushed to open the door for her.

"Thank you." She smiled but knew it didn't reach her eyes.

Sure enough, there was a stretch limo waiting. The driver had the door open, his expression all business.

"You're here from Samuel Dove?"

The driver nodded. "Yes, ma'am." He motioned to the back seat. "You'll find instructions inside."

She gulped. Instructions? She slid into the seat and spotted a note with her name scrawled on top next to a black box. The driver closed the door. Lexi opened the note.

Put this on. She opened the box and found a black blindfold. Part of her wanted to think this was some kind of kinky foreplay and part of her insisted that was wishful thinking. It was more likely that Sam didn't want her to know where he lived. *Fair enough.* She hadn't exactly been great with his secrets before.

She sighed as she slipped the blindfold on, and as tempting as it was to peek, she kept her hands on her lap the entire way. What had to be at least an hour later, maybe longer, she felt the limo turning abruptly onto what sounded like a gravel road or driveway. How far had they come? They were certainly out of the city.

More time passed, with a few bumps along the way, and finally the limo turned again then came to a stop. Lexi so badly wanted to lift her blindfold, but she restrained herself. The door opened and she immediately smelled trees and flowers and maybe even a bit of the beach. It was so lovely that she took in a deep breath and was hit with the scent of Sam.

"Hello, Lexi." Sam's voice was gravelly and gruff. It was a familiar sound that made her toes curl and her heart ramp up. He took her hand as she stepped out of the limo and she shivered. She wanted to wrap her arms around him. She wanted to kiss him.

Instead, she smiled. "Hi, Sam."

"Will that be all, Mr. Dove?"

"Yes, thank you. We'll be in for the rest of the night."

We will? Lexi squeezed Sam's hand—couldn't help herself. Maybe he wasn't going to lecture her on all the ways she'd fucked up his life. Maybe he had other plans.

He didn't say another word as he led her into the house. Her heels echoed on tile floor and she smelled wood polish. Her curiosity was piqued.

He took her down a carpeted flight of stairs, then along another hallway. They paused so he could open a door. "Welcome to my dungeon, Lexi. We've got some things to sort out and you're long overdue for a punishment."

She jolted at the thought of enduring Sam's version of punishment. Her body revved, her nipples hardening and her pussy clenching. A lecture would have been torture—anything else sounded like exactly what she had been missing.

Sam guided her forward, holding her arm lightly as he maneuvered her this way and that. The room smelled of mint and candle wax. Flashes of memory had Lexi vibrating. All the creative torment he'd planned for her when they'd been in their cabin on the yacht had her wondering what surprises he had in store for her now. She was giddy and nearly bursting, desire pulsing through her body, but trusted that whatever Sam had planned would be completely satisfying to her. She knew without a doubt that he would balance that pleasure with the exquisite pain she so badly needed.

"Take off your clothes." His voice was deep, dark and promising dangerous things.

She felt him move away, so she wasn't sure if he was collecting tools or watching her undress. She hoped he couldn't take his eyes off her, because even with a blindfold on, she was a pro at stripping.

It wasn't just the act of unzipping her skirt then sliding the fabric over her hips and down her thighs. It wasn't how she exposed each part of her body for him to see—removing her panties, her tank top, her bra. It wasn't that she left her heels on. All those things were sure to get any man all revved up, his pupils dilated and his hand on his cock, adjusting for the sudden hardness in his pants. She didn't have to see Sam to trust that if he were watching her, which she was certain now that he was, she would see him growing more and more hungry for her. All those things were hot, she knew, but they weren't the thing that would get a man drooling.

It was that Lexi knew how to move. She had been a gymnast, after all.

She knew how to angle her body to show her best form. She knew how to touch herself in all the right places and all the right ways to make a man like Sam want to lay his hands on her and do the same.

She knew he was watching her because she could hear his breathing. He was close, his breath coming hard and fast. She wasn't surprised when he touched her, gripping her arm tightly so he could help her up onto a leather table of some sort. He eased her forward so her front was pressed against the tabletop.

It was cool on her skin but not uncomfortable.

"You using the same safeword?" he whispered against her ear.

She nodded. "Lucky."

He grunted, then set what felt like a large coil of coarse rope on her back. The weight of it was substantial and she knew she'd never be able to break free from it. She shivered. Her body was on fire for this man. It was like he reached into her brain and drew out exactly what she wanted — *no, what I need.*

"This is going to be tight."

As it should be.

Chapter Nineteen

Sam had been practicing his knots. He'd been fantasizing about tying Lexi up, taking control of her with bondage and suspension and ultimately making her scream for all the right reasons.

Yes, he wanted to punish her. She'd broken his trust—to save his life, sure, but still… He owed her and she owed him. He knew this was what she wanted. *No*, what she needed.

He slipped the jute rope around her wrists, tying them. He made sure it was tight enough to cause friction if she wiggled her wrists too much. He lifted her legs, bending them at the knees until her feet almost touched her hands, and was reminded of how flexible she was. She was pliable, completely complacent, just as he expected her to be.

He'd sulked after the fiasco on the yacht because he'd felt like he'd lost so much. Never mind the death of Devon, which had been horrifying by itself, Sam had grieved the loss of his alias and his freedom. Like the spoiled rich man he was raised to be, he'd rejected his father's attempts to reconnect, even while he'd made himself at home in his family's estate, indulging in all the perks his dad's massive wealth afforded him. It had smarted that his father had known all about his alias and had simply been indulging Sam all the years he'd been working at building his career as a reporter. It had frustrated and embarrassed him even more when he'd realized that the massive success he'd achieved was likely because his father had been watching in the wings and probably pulling strings.

It had taken him a week to wise up and snap out of it—a week too long, he was ashamed to admit. While he'd been acting like a man-child, Lexi had been thinking he hated her. He'd left her to deal with the trauma of everything they'd experienced too, which he'd probably never forgive himself for.

It wasn't Lexi's fault that everything had happened the way it had. He'd practically forced her into the situation by including her in all his hastily planned ideas. He'd endangered her too, then to ask her to stay silent about his identity, even in the face of death? Fuck, he could punch himself in the head for being so obtuse and not contacting her sooner.

He pulled the length of rope down and entwined it around her ankles, making sure that it would leave a mark when he cut her loose later. She had every reason to reject him for his behavior, and yet she hadn't. She'd placed her trust in him again, and the fact that she was there, allowing him to tie her up, said everything he needed to know about her feelings for him. Now he was going to show her exactly how deep those feelings were.

He pulled the rope taut enough to raise her shoulders and her thighs off the table by an inch. Her body made a beautiful arc, her nipples barely touching the table. He slipped another rope around her waist, securing her midsection so that she would hang comfortably—or mostly comfortably.

He'd spent some time putting this room together in this house—a house he'd only stepped foot in for the first time three days before. It had been sitting vacant for five years after his father had gifted it to him when he'd graduated from college. Sam remembered how triumphant he'd felt when he'd decided to cut ties to his family. He'd walked away from the wealth his father had offered him and had forged ahead on his own, believing that he was being independent by rejecting everything his family stood for.

When he thought back on it now, he realized he'd been throwing a temper tantrum, all the while knowing that he had a very soft cushion to land on if his writing career didn't work out. His trust fund hadn't gone untouched in the time he'd been living apart from his family. He'd dipped into it as needed, mostly for stories, so he'd thought he was still being rebellious. But all the same, he had never truly separated himself from the luxuries of his former life. He'd just lived in the delusion that he had.

That delusional thinking was over now, and it was time for him to step up and embrace everything that made him Samuel Dove. That didn't mean he was ready to embrace the role his father had created or to suspend his morals and beliefs, the reasons why he'd walked away to begin with. No, it didn't mean that at all. In a moment of clarity, Sam had realized that the only way he would be able to change the path of his family and end the criminal elements that had tainted his family name for decades was to learn the ropes. That way, when the time came, he'd be able to step into the leadership role. Then—and only then—would he be able to make a difference and try to right the wrongs that his father had forged over the years. Of course, he hadn't told his father any of this. He'd simply changed his attitude, opening the door of communication instead of closing it, and had let his father believe that he was ready to fall in line. It was what his father wanted more than anything, so he hadn't questioned Sam's change of attitude. He'd just slapped him on the back and poured him a Scotch.

Sam moved the big metal hooks closer, sliding them along the rails he'd had built into the ceiling.

"Why haven't you accepted Sabine's offer to work as a trainer for the Kitty Cats?" He had three goals for his time with Lexi, and all of them had very selfish links to his own desires and needs.

Lexi scrunched up her face, looking all mystified and sexy. "What? Why?" She tried to move, like she was attempting to look at him, even though she was blindfolded.

"You're depressed, aren't you? That's why you're rejecting the familiar." One by one, he attached the jute rope to the hooks, hoisting Lexi's body up so that she was hovering over the table.

She bit her bottom lip and tried to move but only managed to sway herself on the ropes. "I'm not depressed!" But he knew—and he was certain that she did too—that it was a lie.

"So why not take on the role as trainer?" He moved the table out of the way.

"Because…I…" She let out a huff. "Can we talk about this another time?" *'Or never'*, went without saying.

Sam smiled. "No. We're talking about this now." He picked up the first pair of nipple clamps. "Answer the question." He put the clamps on Lexi's nipple and delighted in the jolt of surprise and the hiss of pain she let out.

"I wouldn't do a good job. I wouldn't do the Kitty Cat name justice."

"Bullshit." He attached the other clamp to the other nipple.

Lexi cried out. These clamps were tight, and he'd only be able to keep them on for a short time. Her nipples were already turning a deep, dark pink. "I'm not the same person I was," she said frantically.

"Because you're depressed." He picked up the vibrator from the table next to him and turned it on. Lexi's whole body trembled.

"I can't do the things I used to do."

"Okay, that's fair." He moved the vibrator along her skin, slowly working his way down her body. "But Sabine is offering you a way to reinvent yourself."

"Why do you care, anyway?" she snapped. For that, she needed to be punished.

He put the vibrator against her clit, sucking any more words right out of her mouth. She arched her back even more and moaned. Her whole body shook. He flicked her clamped nipples, then squeezed her breasts, causing her to buck wildly.

"I care because I know how much you love being a Kitty Cat and working for Sabine." He moved away from her, releasing her suddenly, leaving her to sway.

"It will never be the same, though." She shook her head.

Sam moved the vibrator back to her clit. Lexi rolled her hips as best as she could. Her expression was desperate, and he could tell that if he left the vibrator there for another minute, she would totally come. So of course, he pulled it away.

"What do you want from me?" she groaned. "What do you want me to say?"

Sam quickly removed the clamps then put the vibrator there, alternating between her nipples. Lexi's mouth opened but no sound came out. She squeezed her thighs together and her whole body swayed on the ropes.

"I want you to say that you'll get some help for your depression. I want you to say that you'll reconsider Sabine's offer." He put the clamps down and picked up the cat o' nine tails. It was made out of leather, and it could leave quite a sting if he wanted it to.

Lexi didn't say anything, so he brought the cat o' nine tails to slap against the underside of her tits. One hit. Two hits — using enough force that she winced but not enough to raise welts.

"Yes, yes. I will. I'll get help."

Sam stopped hitting her and grabbed her face in his hand. He brought her close to him and kissed her with everything he had. She melted into him, her tongue clearly eager for his, her mouth devouring his. When he pulled back, he didn't let go of her face.

"And I will too. I'll get a therapist to help me with my issues." Because there were issues — not only as a result of the trauma from what he'd experienced on the yacht, but also all his bullshit angst that needed straightening out. Sam reached up and released the hook that was holding her legs in place. Her body dropped down by a foot. He grabbed a chair and sat himself at pussy level.

"I'll talk to Sabine again." Lexi panted.

Sam grinned. "Good girl." He put his hands on her ass and brought her toward him. His breath was ragged, his cock so hard it was throbbing. He wanted to pound her sweet pussy, but that would come in time. He pushed her knees apart, then ran his tongue along her glistening slit.

She shook on the ropes, her tits jiggling beautifully.

"I thought you should know that I'm working for Cowan Enterprises." He said this as he clamped his lips around her clit and sucked that sweet nub so hard that he didn't know if Lexi's cry of surprise was at his words or his actions.

Probably both.

He spent some time licking and sucking, rolling his tongue against her clit, savoring the juice that mingled with his saliva. He slipped his fingers inside her, pumping so that he was hitting her G-spot.

Once he got her really writhing, he pulled his mouth away and stilled his fingers. "She called me. Sabine, that is." He enjoyed watching Lexi's face go through the emotions of realizing he wasn't going to work her clit, then hearing his words and that information registering on her face. "She made me an offer I couldn't refuse."

"W-w-what offer?"

He got up from the chair then moved around her. "She told me that a man with my family connections and writing ability would be a strong asset to her company." He unzipped his pants. "And I agreed." He slipped a condom on then gripped Lexi's hips. "My father was in favor as well. He thinks I'll learn a lot from a woman as business-savvy as Sabine—and I agree. So, starting next week, I'm going to be working on some confidential shit for Cowan Enterprises." He nudged her slick pussy with his dick. "And I'd love to be able to tell you about it, but you're not a Kitty Cat anymore." He let that sink in.

Her whole body was tense. "Sam," she moaned.

"No one thinks you're broken, Lexi, except you." He pushed into her, one thrust, spearing her pussy until his balls slapped against her flesh.

She groaned and he could hear her satisfaction in that sound. He held her hip with one hand then reached forward so he could pinch her nipple. He drew himself back, then slammed her again.

"My father and Sabine have formed an alliance. He's merging his film company with her brand." Sam continued to fuck Lexi as he talked. "She's closer to being a super-power of the sex industry. She needs you to be part of the team."

"I don't know how." Lexi grunted out her words. "I don't know how to be that person anymore."

"And yet the first chance you got to be a Kitty Cat again and work as a spy for Sabine, you jumped at it. You say you're ready to move on, but we both know you're not." Sam stopped moving. His cock rested inside Lexi, pulsing with his heartbeat. It was killing him not to move, but he knew it was killing Lexi more.

"I said I'd go to therapy! I said I'd talk to Sabine! What more do you want from me?"

"I want you to promise it to me." Sam pulled his dick out slowly.

They both knew what he was asking. Lexi didn't break promises, not unless it was life or death. "Sam...I can't."

He pulled all the way out of her.

Lexi couldn't say those words. She couldn't make another promise to Sam. Was she depressed? Yes! Of course, she was. She'd suffered a catastrophic injury that had ended her life in so many ways. She'd been grieving the loss for over a year. And it was all made worse by having not only witnessing Devon's murder but being the reason he'd died in the first place. If she'd only accessed the database instead of mouthing off to Dax...

"You have demons. I have them too." He leaned over her and kissed her shoulder. "We need to tame them so they don't control us anymore, so our life decisions aren't rooted in our fear of those demons slipping out. Lexi," he whispered as he trailed his hands down her front, stopping just short of her pussy. "Promise me you'll take the steps to free yourself — and I'll do the same."

"I thought you liked my demons." Her voice was raw. Her brain was so fuzzy that she couldn't understand his words. Was he saying that he wanted her to change? Was he saying she wasn't good enough?

"I love you, Lexi. I'll take you in whatever way you come, but I think you know as well as I do that these demons we carry with us are doing more damage than good. They don't define us...never did."

She nodded. No, her demons had only come after her accident, after the betrayal by her coach, by her league. "But we're not going to stop the pain play, right?" Because liking the pain had come at the expense of her back injury, but she wouldn't change that for anything.

"Ohhhh, baby…" He slipped his fingers to her clit and pressed down hard. "Our pain play will be in our pre-nup."

She gasped. *What is he saying?* "Are you serious?"

"Nah." He rubbed her clit vigorously.

Her hope deflated, but her body revved up and her climax mounted. Why would he want to marry a girl like her anyway?

"I won't make you sign a pre-nup. The pain play will be assumed." He pumped his cock in fast and hard, pulling a long moan out of her as all coherent thought exploded, along with her orgasm.

She saw stars, truly, and came so hard that she was sure she was about to die. Wave upon wave of intense pleasure made her legs melt and her body shake. Sam roared as he climaxed, bucking against her so violently that her arms were chafing against the rope, and she loved it… She loved it all.

"Promise me," he growled, just before he bit down hard on her shoulder, riding her through every pulse and spasm of his cock.

She cried out. "Yes, yes, I promise. I promise!"

Epilogue

"I have a training session to run in thirty minutes." Lexi was only half-trying to push herself away from Sam. The truth was, she loved it when he barged into her office to ravage her.

"That's all the time I need, baby," he said as he kissed along her collarbone. His hands were all over her, squeezing her breasts, running down her body, cupping her ass.

"I got a call from a bank in the Cayman Islands today." Lexi felt a knot in her throat. "They wanted to know what I wanted to do with the account Devon Caldone had created for me." She pulled back a bit. Her stomach did a little drop. "One-point-five million." She swallowed. "I didn't think he'd actually done it. I mean, that he actually followed through on his end of the deal."

Sam ran his hand through her hair then pulled her into his chest. "Devon was a dick at the best of times, but he never fell through on a deal. If he owed money for something, he always paid up. Besides, what was a million or two to him anyway? The guy was loaded."

"Right, but I don't know what to do with it. I mean, it was my fault—"

"Nah, remember what your therapist told you about that." Sam rubbed her back gently.

Lexi checked herself. "I didn't pull the trigger."

"No, you didn't. And the person who did paid for that decision with his life."

"But the money…"

"Is yours. Keep it in a high-yield account so you can use the interest if you want."

Lexi nodded, still not convinced. "Maybe I can give it away."

"You could." He pulled her back so he could look at her. "Or you could keep it there, never touch it and live off my money for the rest of your life." He grinned. "That way you'll never feel like you're trapped. You're independently wealthy all on your own."

Lexi swatted him. "I'll never feel trapped."

"With a family like I have, you never know." Sam laughed as he pulled her in for another hug, followed by an ass groping.

She knew he was joking, but all the same, she felt compelled to say it again. "I will never feel trapped. You and I are meant to be together."

"Hell yeah, we are." Sam nodded. "What toy are you introducing to the new Kitty Cats today?"

Lexi laughed. "So that's what you're after." She managed to disentangle herself. "You knew a shipment came in, didn't you?"

Sam's hair was tussled a bit and his shirt crumpled where she'd pulled it out of his pants. He looked adorable in a bad boy, sexy-as-fuck way. "I was chatting with Vivian. She might have mentioned some new sexy stuff." He wagged his eyebrows.

Lexi sighed in an exaggerated way. "Okay, sit down." She walked to the other side of the room. "No peeking!"

Sam did as he was told and sat down in the lounge chair on the other side of her desk. He covered his eyes. "Promise, no peeking."

Lexi rolled her eyes. She could see Sam's pupils through his splayed fingers. "My lesson plan today is costume play. We're introducing new Kitty Cat wear that is going to rock the socks off the Gentlemen's Club."

Sam nodded but didn't say anything. She knew he had the patience of a teenager when it came to sex — not that she minded. He was all kinds of wonderful, and not only because he fucked her good every damn day.

She'd already set aside the costume she was going to wear to class for the new girls to see. What better way to know how it would go over than testing it out on Sam?

"Since you're not going to close your eyes, do you want to help me with this instead?" She was unbuttoning her blouse as she spoke.

Sam dropped his hands and jumped up from the chair. "You bet I do!" He came rushing over. "I heard there's a butt plug with a tail!" He swatted her hands away so he could finish unbuttoning her.

Lexi laughed. "Among other things."

Not one to waste time when it came to sex, Sam helped her get undressed quickly. He even tore her panties a little in his haste to get her naked. He also kissed her up and down, pulled a few moans out of her before he was done helping.

"Okay, where's the butt plug?" Sam rubbed his hands together.

Lexi pulled the long black-and-white tail out of her carrying case. It was silky and ended with a good-sized metal butt plug. "Grab the lube from my desk?"

Sam rushed to do as she asked. While he was rooting through her drawer, Lexi put the cat-ear headband on, then picked up the studded collar.

She walked toward Sam, the collar dangling from her fingers and the butt plug in her other hand.

"Found it!" He held up the bottle of lube like he'd just pulled the sword out of the stone. His pupils dilated when he saw her, his mouth hanging open a bit. "Is that what I think it is?"

She twirled the collar on her finger. "It comes with a leash."

Sam moaned. "Oh, baby, this is going to be so hot."

She held both hands out. "Which one first?"

He moved around her desk, dropping the lube on top before snatching the collar out of her hand. "You want me to put this on you? You know what it means, right?"

Lexi looked up at him through her eyelashes and bit her bottom lip. She nodded, her breath catching a little. Yes, she knew what it meant. "I want you to collar me, Sam."

He pulled her into his arms and crushed his lips onto hers. When Sam kissed her, it was like a first kiss. It always took her breath away. It made her toes curl, did funny things to her heart and her whole body went into insta-insatiable lust.

She was moaning by the time he broke their kiss. Her body was tingling as he put the collar around her throat. Her heart was doing flip-flops. He held her gaze, their eyes locked and she saw everything she felt shining right back at her.

"You're mine, Lexi," his voice was gravelly.

"Forever," she said.

The collar was tight — not too tight that she couldn't breathe, but tight enough that she wouldn't forget it was there. She lifted the butt plug and Sam took it from her hands.

He reached behind him to grab the lube and Lexi turned so she could offer up her ass. It didn't completely shock her when she felt the heavy smack of his palm on her ass cheek, but she yelped all the same. Sam's spankings were intense, and she loved every swat he gave her, even if she'd be feeling it all through her training lesson. She liked the reminder of him and absolutely loved when he left a handprint behind.

He smacked her two more times — same place, same intensity — until she had tears in her eyes from the sting. When he stopped, she braced herself for the plug. It was bigger than anything she'd put in her ass up until now, but she wasn't nervous.

"I've always wanted to do this to you." Sam teased her asshole with his finger, lubing her before he slicked up the metal plug. "You ready for it?"

Lexi shifted so she could brace herself against the bookshelf, clenching the wood with enough force that her knuckles turned white. "Yes. Do it."

Sam eased the plug in, pushing gently before giving her a break, then doing it again until finally the plug slid in past the ring of muscles. He put it in deep, and her ass gripped it tightly. It was bigger than she'd thought once it was inside. It made her feel full and her body pulsed with a new kind of sensation. Sam swished the tail so that the soft fur tickled her ass cheeks. "Stand up, little Kitty."

Lexi did as she was told, giving her body time to adjust the new position. The plug was nestled in and she felt it every time she moved. It sparked a different kind of lust in her. "There are nipple clamps."

Sam's eyebrows shot up as he turned to the bag. He fished around and pulled out the chain leash and the nipple clamps. "They have bells on them."

Lexi grinned. "Yep."

Sam didn't waste any time. He clamped her nipples, which made her gasp because they were damn tight, then to torture her more, he flicked the bells so they jingled. "Ohhh, yeah, I like these." He grinned like a madman. "On your hands and knees, Kitty." He hooked the leash onto the collar just before Lexi did as he'd commanded.

Sam moved back to the chair then sat down, his hand still on the leash. He tugged her forward. "Come up onto my lap, pretty girl."

Lexi crawled toward him. The carpet abraded her knees. The butt plug caused each move she made to be more deliberate. The tail swished from side to side. Her nipple clamps chimed each time she moved forward. She locked her eyes on his, reveling in the dark and dangerous lust she saw there.

She got up on her knees and Sam wrapped the leash around his hand, tightening his hold and pulling her closer. He widened his legs so she could move in between them. She licked her lips and watched with rapt attention as he unzipped his pants for her. His cock was hard and weeping pre-cum.

"I've been thinking about your lips all day, Lexi." His voice was rough, and he looked at her with deep need.

She leaned in, her breath coming hard and fast, her stomach doing flips because she loved sucking Sam's cock. She ran her tongue up his length like she was licking a Popsicle. Sam sucked in a deep breath and readjusted his position, shifting his body down a bit. Lexi moved closer, wedging her body more tightly between his legs. She lifted her hands to grasp his dick at the same time that she lowered her lips over his tip.

"Yes," he hissed.

She moved up so she could slide her mouth down, taking him all the way to the back of her throat. He was so big that her lips were stretched to their limit. She moved her hands to his balls, cupping them gently while she worked her jaw, so she could take his cock down her throat.

He moaned when she took him down the rest of the way, then moaned again when she hummed softly. He put his hand in her hair, gripping tightly so that her scalp pulled and she would have cried out if her mouth wasn't so full.

"You drive me crazy, Lexi." Sam's eyes were hooded and his voice was strained. He tugged her hair as she was about to go down on him again. "No. That's enough. I need your pussy. *Now*."

He let go of her hair and pulled her leash. She climbed up onto his lap. He flicked her clamps so the bells rang and her nipples throbbed. "I'll never get tired of that."

She arched her back slightly, her pussy grazed against his cock. "I want to ride you."

"Mmm-hmmm," he said as he put his hands on her hips and guided her closer.

They'd both been tested and cleared, so condoms were no longer necessary. Lexi rolled her hips down. She loved the feel of Sam's bare cock and the feel of his cum filling her up. She shifted down slowly as Sam held his dick, easing inside her. The butt plug was pushing against her pussy on one side and Sam's cock was pushing on the other. Slowly...slowly, she took him all the way in.

"You okay?" He grunted his words, his eyes half-closed and a look of bliss on his face.

"Yes, *so* okay." She took a second to adjust to having both holes filled with hard, unyielding things. She was riding that line between pain and pleasure, and she couldn't have been happier.

Sam lifted her, moving her hips up until his cock was almost out of her body. He locked eyes with her when she reached his tip. Staring at him, knowing what was coming, Lexi sucked in a deep breath. "Do it."

He rammed her down, hard, fast, then lifted her back up again. Even with her on top, he took the lead, using his strong arms to move her on his dick. She rolled her hips as best as she could, but she was too caught up in the sensations. Her pussy was rippling, her G-spot ready to explode, her nipples on fire. There was so much going on that she couldn't form coherent thought. All she wanted was *moremoremore*.

She heard herself moan like she was having an out-of-body experience. Sam lifted his hands, giving her control over how she moved. She was so close...so damn close...that she slowed things down, savoring the moments as her climax gained strength, building and building.

Sam released her nipples at the same time. The bells on the clamps tinkled. The rush of blood to her nipples made her scream, and in that moment, her orgasm crested.

Sam had his hands on her hips once again, and with a few more thrusts, he was climaxing right along with her, filling her up with hot spurts of cum and moaning through its intensity.

She collapsed into his chest, resting her head on his shoulder. "You always know what I need when I need it." Her pussy still quivered around his cock.

He rubbed his hands down her back then gave a little tug on her tail. "So, you gonna tell the new Kitty Cats how the product testing went?"

"Of course! Firsthand experience is the best teacher, but I like to give them graphic details of how the products worked for me."

Sam groaned. "No wonder those girls are always smirking and whispering when they see me."

Lexi smiled against his chest. "They know who you are. They think you're a gangster and that's hot. You could snap your fingers and have any one of them."

"Well, there's only one Kitty Cat I want." He reached down then squeezed her ass. "And only one woman I'd be willing to product test with."

Lexi curled herself into him. "That's good, because I belong to you."

He tugged her leash and nuzzled her. "That's right. You're mine, Lexi—now and forever."

Want to see more from this author?
Here's a taster for you to enjoy!

Wicked Distractions:
Wicked Trouble
Angela Addams

Coming Spring 2022

Excerpt

Cammie didn't do vacations very well, mostly because she loathed stepping away from the love of her life…work. But when the uber-powerful Sabine Cowan insisted on an all-expenses paid kink cruise, what she called *"mandatory R and R"*, what was a girl supposed to do?

A hardcore type-A like Cammie played to her strengths, so that's what she did. She packed her bags and made a cruise 'to-do' list. One, schmooze and network more Kitty Cat connections—Gentlemen's Club candidates, Kitty Cat hopefuls and new clients. Two, product test, because, come on…a kink cruise? *A girl's gotta have a little fun at work.* Three, get laid…repeatedly. *It is a vacation after all…even if it's forced.* It'd been a looong time since she'd found a man to crank her little kink-loving heart.

"This will be your cabin, Miss. Sheppard. Your boss really loves you." Ben, her steward, winked like they were already best friends. He'd been effervescent the entire way to her stateroom, bubbling with energy and peppering her with questions about where she'd travelled from and what she hoped to do on the five-day cruise. It had been impossible not to get caught up in his enthusiasm as he pumped up the various events that had been planned. "Shall I put your bags in the closet?"

A walk-in closet? In a stateroom? "Yes, please. Thank you, Ben."

Of course, Sabine had spared no expense, so Cammie's cabin was beyond luxurious. It was larger than her own bedroom at home in New York and big enough for a king-size bed, a lounge-dining area and a restroom that included an actual whirlpool tub. The view was spectacular as well. With floor-to-ceiling windows along one wall, Cammie would be able to see miles of ocean with no obstructed views. She also had a balcony and pictured herself having her morning coffee there while she checked email and knocked a few things off her 'non-cruise to-do list', of course.

"Is there anything else I can do for you, Miss. Sheppard?" Ben stood at the door, his hands folded in front of him and his face clearly eager to please. His blond hair flopped over one eye, giving him an adorably disheveled look.

"Oh gosh, no. I'm fine." She dug out some money from her purse then handed it to him. "Thanks for getting me here safe and sound. This ship is so huge I think it'll take me five days just to get the hang of where everything is." Which was a total lie… Cammie had the entire ship mapped out from bow to stern and everything in between before she'd stepped foot on board.

"I'm here if you need me. Just pick up the phone and I'll answer." Ben slipped the cash into his pocket with a nod and a grin. "Don't forget about the sunset mixer on the Sky Deck."

Cammie rubbed her hands together. "I'll be there!" A sunset mixer sounded like exactly the type of place she'd find people to network with.

She had an hour to get ready, so she pulled out her sun-and-fun mixer dress, an orange, yellow and pink strapless that hugged her curves just right, then headed into the massive restroom for a dip in the tub. If Sabine wanted her to relax, she could at least make an effort.

It turned out that networking was easier than finding a non-alcoholic cocktail on the Sky Deck. Cammie had been offered no less than four umbrella-adorned drinks by four different scantily clad servers, and each time she'd asked if it was possible to get a soda or even water, she'd only been met with looks of confusion before a mumbled, "Of course! Let me get that for you." She'd yet to find a cold drink in her hand, but she had met three very eligible men, who had been eagerly listening to what she had to say about the Kitty Cat Gentlemen's Club. They hadn't even balked at the fee range she'd hinted at.

"You can sign me up, little lady." Mr. William Haversmith wore a huge tan cowboy hat on his huge head. Everything about the man was larger than life, from his booming laugh and his ridiculously large cowboy boots to his long, curled mustache. "In fact, a pretty little thing like you can do whatever she wants with my assets." He winked.

"Bill, don't you know woman don't like to be spoken to like that?" Elm Stone also wore a cowboy hat and towered over Cammie in the same way his friend did, which wasn't hard considering Cammie was a whopping five foot three inches. He tried to come off as more gentlemanly, even though Cammie had witnessed him slip his hands over several of the servers' asses as they passed by.

"I'm sorry. Can't help myself. You're a tiny, sexy thing, though. And on a naughty cruise like this to boot! You're a firecracker, aren't you? I can see it in your eyes." He winked again and Cammie had to wonder if he had a tic or if he really did think she — or any woman, really — was into his kind of flirting. "And those dimples! So cute! I could just eat you up." He leaned closer. "You don't mind if I call you 'little lady', do you, sweetheart?"

Did she mind? *Hell yes!* But she'd never say that out loud. Working in an industry that catered to men, she'd become used to the ways that men behaved and the condescending things they often said. "Of course not, Mr. Haversmith." She grinned, making sure her dimples popped for him. "I'm just going to charge you more for your membership."

The men all laughed in their hearty way, not believing for one second that she would, in fact, give them the elevated price she reserved for special men like him. She laughed too, but hers — if a person listened closely — was edged with a 'fuck you'.

"Well, you've got my contact information. Be sure to put it to good use, honey." He didn't wink again, *thank goodness*, but he did waggle his eyebrows like he was sending some kind of secret message.

Cammie laughed again then waved him off. "If you'll excuse me, gentlemen, I'm going to search out a drink. I'm absolutely parched!" She didn't stick around for another suggestive comment, but the men's laughter and what could only be described as catcalls did follow her as she moved through the crowd.

Ugh.

"Oh, there you are!" A tall redhead wearing a super-flattering black, skin hugging, leather dress rushed to her on four-inch stilettos with a frosty glass in hand. "Soda water for you. I added a lime just in case you wanted a bit of flavor."

"Thank you!" The timing couldn't have been more perfect. Cammie really was dying of thirst.

"Soda water, huh?"

She turned toward the gravelly voice like a puppet on a string. "Yeah, I'm not into alcohol."

"Smart. Don't want to get too drunk then end up tied down and at some Dom's mercy." The guy standing next to her checked all Cammie's eye-candy boxes. He was tall and wide, barrel-chested, thick-armed and, like her, appeared to enjoy food. "That's why I'm only sipping my beer."

"Bound and at the mercy of a Dom is exactly how I want to end up." A bold statement, sure, but Cammie had a to-do list and this guy might be her way to check off one of those bullet points.

"Zane," he said, one eyebrow raised.

Amused or intrigued? It was hard to tell. He tilted his pint glass toward hers.

"Cammie." She turned herself toward him so she could take in his full size then clinked her glass with his. She liked men with meat on them. They complemented her curves and were usually hefty enough to hoist her into the positions she loved. "You here alone?"

His eyes crinkled and a grin tugged his lips. "Are you hitting on me?"

"Not yet." Cammie grinned back.

"Oh…dimples, how very —"

"If you say cute, I'm leaving." Cammie took a sip from her glass, watching him over the jutting lime. Her body heat had to be wafting off her with the way her pussy quivered and wept. Zane was exactly the kind of guy she could have some fun with.

Get laid-- check!

"Enticing." He gave her a spicy once-over, trailing a hot as hell gaze down, lingering over her double d's to the curve of her extra wide hips then back up again. "Yes, I'm here alone."

"I'm not looking for love." Cammie would never be accused of beating around the bush, especially not when it came to sex.

"Neither am I."

* * * *

Smack!

Cammie's ass burned like a thousand suns, and she was sure that Zane's handprint would be seared into her flesh before he was done with her. He had taken her over his knee, and, as she'd correctly guessed, he was hefty enough to lift then hold her there while he squeezed her dangling tits and walloped her cheeks with his open palm. Neither of them had wasted time stripping, and his hearty cock was digging into her stomach, nudging her every time Zane reeled back for another hit. She would have liked to rub his shaft, but he'd expertly tied her hands behind her back using her bra, and she wasn't in a position to maneuver his cock into her mouth. She was at this bear's mercy, just as she liked it.

Not for the first time, Zane seemed to read her mind. He heaved her off his lap then positioned her on her knees. He spread his legs, his cock jutting massively at mouth level. "Let me see those dimples pop, dirty girl."

She grinned as she opened her mouth then gulped down his dick, pressing her tongue firmly to his shaft as he eased his way in. She gagged and he pulled back, but she shook her head, opened her mouth wider, shifted forward, then took him all the way into her throat.

He growled like a predator that was hungry for more. She sucked him as she moved all the way back to his tip, her lips pressed around his head, flicking her tongue along the ridge of his crown. He reached down to fondle her breasts, pulling a yelp out of her as he pinched and pulled her nipples until her eyes watered.

She swallowed his cock, taking him to the hilt, then slowly backing off again. He smacked her tits with a sharp slap, angling to hit the sides so that they slammed together. He'd squeeze them then, gripping hard, before moving back to her nipples, tweaking and taunting all over again.

He spurted a drop of cum, like a preshow to the big explosion, and Cammie swallowed it greedily. She wanted more but he pushed her back so forcefully that she landed on her sore ass with a thump and moaned through the smarting pain.

"We're coming together." He lifted her by the underarms, then flipped her over, shoving her face-down into the mattress.

She heard more than saw him rip open a condom package and her core coiled. She lifted her ass and buried her face into the comforter.

Smack!

Her ass burned all over again. She gulped down a scream.

Smack!

She rocked forward on a groan.

He nudged her legs wider, slipped his hand around her waist and hoisted her up and back, before spearing her completely with his giant dick.

She gasped but he gave her no time to adjust. Instead, he swatted her ass again and again, each hit punctuated by a thrust of his rock-hard member.

He reached around and rubbed her clit, sending explosive sparks through her body. Her toes curled and her pussy spasmed. She dug her shoulder into the bed to keep her face from being smothered and gazed over her shoulder to watch this beast of a man ram her. He rocked her with his powerful thrusts, teased her into a frenzy with his fingers circling her clit so roughly and, somehow, continued to tan her ass, alternating between sides until she was sure she'd never be able to sit again.

His cock was a steel rod — hard, slick and punishing as he drilled her relentlessly. Her self-control was no match for his unwavering attention, so when her orgasm crested, holding back was impossible. There'd be no delayed gratification today. Her climax spasmed through her with a full body quiver, then cascaded like a rocket launcher, shooting blast after blast until she was crying out through each shockwave. Zane bellowed through his orgasm, grunting and groaning with each thrust until he collapsed to his knees, his cock sliding out of her pussy before she was completely finished with him. He kissed her sore ass cheeks, and his tenderness made her knees wobble.

She shifted to her side, too scared to put weight on her ass right away and looked down at him. He brushed his fingers through his hair, pushing it from his face as he puffed out his breaths.

"You done?" she asked with a quirk of her lips. "Or are you hungry for more?"

His eyes narrowed in that sexy hooded way men have. "I'm always hungry for more."

"I think every cabin has suspension gear in the closet." She motioned to his smaller, more cost-efficient space where some of his clothes appeared to be hanging. His cabin was several floors down from hers and was more like a dorm room — tight space and plain decor. "I don't think I'll be able to sit for a while."

"I'm good at tying knots." Zane pulled the condom from his cock before standing. "And there are hooks all over this room." Which made the tight space all-the-more appealing. He could literally suspend her over the bed if he wanted — and she definitely wanted.

"Then I think we're in for a really fun night."

* * * *

Somehow, in the haze of her post-climax buzz, Cammie found her way through the maze of decks to her cabin. It was too early for anyone to be out and about. Even the crew was virtually non-existent at three a.m. Cammie was very much looking forward to pouring herself into bed and sleeping the rest of the morning away. *Breakfast be damned*. Her appetite had been satiated already — repeatedly, in fact.

She slipped her key card into the reader, thankful when it beeped without a fuss, then slipped quietly into her room. The view of the ocean and how it kissed the star-infused night sky was breathtaking. Cammie didn't bother turning on the lights. She could see the bed and that was the only destination she had in mind.

She took a few steps then stumbled, her foot catching on something solid next to the bed. Luckily, she braced herself on the night table so she didn't hit the floor.

"What the…?" She flicked on the light and shifted an annoyed look to whatever had tripped her.

Then she choked on a scream.

Lying next to her bed, on the floor, was a man. He was on his back, his face slack, his mouth gaping and his eyes wide and vacant.

He was clearly, very definitely dead.

Home of Erotic Romance

Sign up for our newsletter and find out about all our romance book releases, eBook sales and promotions, sneak peeks and FREE romance books!

About the Author

Angela Addams is an author of many naughty things. She believes that the written word is an amazing tool for crafting the most erotic of scenarios and likes telling stories about normal people getting down and dirty and falling in love. Enthralled by the paranormal at an early age, Angela also spends a lot of her time thinking up new story ideas that involve supernatural creatures in everyday situations.

She is an avid tattoo collector, a total book hoarder, and loves anything covered in chocolate…except for bugs. She lives in Ontario, Canada in an old, creaky house, with her husband, children and four moody cats.

Angela loves to hear from readers. You can find her contact information, website details and author profile page at https://www.totallybound.com